'I'll be here, Sydney. I'm not going anywhere.'

'Noah—could you…? Would you hold me? Just… hold me. I'll be strong tomorrow, I promise. Tonight, I just need to be held. Please.'

He knew he was going to do as she asked, even though he'd be tempting fate to its limit. Careful to keep his body outside the bedcovers, he pulled her against his chest.

She nestled against him. He wanted to groan in frustration.

'I know you'll find this hard to believe,' she mumbled, 'but I'm not usually this weak.'

Weak? She thought she was weak? 'I think you're one tough lady, Syd.'

'Good,' she muttered sleepily. 'Have to be strong…to deal with a man like you.'

Soon her breathing deepened. Noah watched the steady rise and fall of her chest, glad he'd covered her excuse for a nightgown with a blanket. He should get up and go to his own bed like a gentleman. But he wasn't feeling very gentlemanly.

'Don't worry, Syd,' he whispered. She didn't stir. He could feel her soft breath on his shirt. 'You and the baby are mine to protect. No one is going to hurt you ever again.'

Dear Reader,

Welcome to this month's selection of Intrigues, and what an exciting month we have for you!

First, rising star Gayle Wilson returns with another of her ever-popular SECRET WARRIORS novels; *Midnight Remembered* is the last in the current series about former agents with new identities.

There's more mystery and suspense in our latest mini-series SECRET IDENTITY, where Debbi Rawlins gives us *Her Mysterious Stranger*—a sexy lawyer who is not what he appears to be meets his match with feisty Taryn Scott!

This month's LAWMAN LOVER is protective, sexy Sheriff Reese Walker from Carla Cassidy's *Fugitive Father*; he's discovered he's a father, and that his daughter and her mother are in danger—and he isn't going to lose them again!

Finally, Dani Sinclair returns with *My Baby, My Love*. Sydney Edwards woke up in hospital pregnant, a widow, the only witness to a murder and with a handsome man gazing down at her, vowing to protect her at all costs…

Enjoy!

The Editors

My Baby, My Love
DANI SINCLAIR

First published in Great Britain 2001
Silhouette Books, Eton House, 18-24 Paradise Road,
Richmond, Surrey TW9 1SR

© Patricia A Gagne 2000

ISBN 0 373 22551 2

46-0801

Printed and bound in Spain
by Litografía Rosés S.A., Barcelona

DANI SINCLAIR

An avid reader, Dani Sinclair never took her own writing seriously until her only sister caught her between career moves and asked her to write a romance novel. Dani quickly discovered she could combine her love of action/adventure with a dash of humour while creating characters who find love together despite the odds. Dani lives in a Maryland suburb outside of Washington, DC, a place she's found to be a great source for both intrigue and humour!

Dear Reader,

In *My Baby, My Love*, I bring you Sydney and Noah's story. Sydney is a sophisticated woman, used to taking care of herself. Though city raised, she appreciates the peace of a small community. Fools Point looks like an ideal setting for a single woman to raise her baby. After school, Noah severed his connection to the quiet town, opting to make the military his life. He never anticipated returning, until his brother died, leaving behind a pregnant widow and a tie Noah can't sever. Their lives are about to change, and nothing will ever be the same again.

Happy Reading!

Dani Sinclair

For Rhonda Harding Pollero (goddess extraordinaire) for unstinting help, unwavering friendship and incredible talent. Best five dollar investment I ever made.

And always, for Roger, Chip, Dan and Barb, who never fail to be there for me.

Prologue

Her heart thudded in her chest. Despite the early-morning hour, Jerome's red sports car was already in the parking lot behind the bank. Fear of another confrontation with her husband nearly made Sydney get back in her car and drive away.

Then she spotted Mrs. Argossy. The bank manager was struggling to hang on to a dozen balloons while lifting a case of soda from the trunk of her car. Jerome wouldn't start a scene in front of his boss. Not when he was up for promotion again. All Sydney had to do was stay near Mrs. Argossy and she could start the morning without a battle. And maybe if she saw him early and got it over with, he wouldn't disrupt the jewelry store where she worked by coming over at lunch.

"Need some help?" she called out.

"Sydney! Good morning! Some help would be wonderful."

"Someone's birthday?" she asked.

"Janet's. We're going to have a party after work this afternoon. I thought I'd get a jump on things by bringing my contribution early, but I see Jerome is already here. You two certainly do get up early for a pair of newly-weds."

Sydney tried to slow the nervous hammering of her pulse by-taking the case of soda and reaching for a gallon of ice cream. Gratefully, Mrs. Argossy lifted a gaily decorated cake and shut the trunk.

"We're hardly newlyweds," Sydney said quietly. She didn't add that they were about to become divorce statistics as soon as she met with her lawyer.

Mrs. Argossy had to set down the cake to unlock the bank doors. She repeated the process once more before they were inside. Empty, the place looked eerie to Sydney. She trailed after Mrs. Argossy past the counters to the rear of the building. There she had to wait again while Mrs. Argossy unlocked yet another set of doors.

Sydney had never been back in this area and she stepped inside curiously. A curse rent the air.

"You said we'd be alone," a male voice accused harshly.

Sydney came to a startled halt. A man twisted away from her, ducking to hide his features. He pulled a ski mask into place before Sydney could register the wrongness of his presence here inside the closed bank.

A second man, stuffing currency inside a large gym bag, also wore a mask over his face. The vault gaped wide open. Jerome stood beside the heavy steel door, several bundles of money in his hands.

Fear stole her vocal cords, leaving her motionless with shock.

"For heaven's sake," Mrs. Argossy chided behind Sydney, unaware of the danger. "Keep moving or I'll drop this cake."

The ski-masked stranger swore viciously. "What are you doing in here?"

Sydney managed the fleeting thought that it was a rather stupid question under the circumstances. Then Jerome started in her direction, his expression almost tortured. For a second, their eyes locked. She felt his anguish as clearly as if he'd cried out.

The door closed behind Mrs. Argossy. In slow motion, her lips formed a wide "oh" of alarm. "What on earth?"

Sydney dropped the heavy case of soda and cans spilled across the floor. Two split open, splashing their sticky contents everywhere.

Mrs. Argossy pushed past her. Feeling helplessly detached, Sydney watched the first man produce a gun in one gloved hand. Smoke and flame spit from the barrel. The bark of noise was deafening. Mrs. Argossy crumpled bonelessly to the floor at Sydney's feet in a pool of spreading red blood. The balloons she'd been holding drifted toward the ceiling.

"No! Stop!" Jerome yelled. "You said no one would be hurt!"

Sydney came out of her panicked stupor. She heaved the gallon of ice cream at the weapon now aimed at her. The container struck, deflecting the next shot.

The room seemed to swell with noise and an acrid odor. There was no place to run. Pain seared Sydney's hand.

The gunman took aim again. Jerome stumbled, shoving her backward. Flame spurted from the weapon.

His body jerked, once—then twice. His mouth opened for another protest that never came.

She lurched as Jerome's full weight collapsed against her. His body jerked again as more bullets thudded into his back.

They fell amid the rain of currency fluttering from his limp hands. Her world dissolved with a blinding crack of pain and a stab of brilliant light.

Chapter One

Sydney woke to the scent of something elusive, something intriguing, something that wafted past the smell of flowers and antiseptic. In an effort to find the source, she forced open her eyes and tried to focus on the face that hovered above her.

"Sydney? That's it, open your eyes. Can you hear me?"

The rumbly voice was comforting. She'd heard that voice in her dreams. A voice that promised safety and security from the nightmares.

Memory flooded her with violent images.

Sydney opened her mouth, a scream building from her soul. The man shook his head. His fingers pressed gently against her raw, chapped lips.

"Don't," he ordered. "You're safe now. You don't have to scream anymore."

The tone, rather than the words, released the scream as a long shuddering sigh. Sydney trembled. Pain raced up her arm. Other pain quickly followed. She tried to lift her hand. It wouldn't move. Something white covered it completely. Sydney fought against the incipient panic rising in her chest.

She couldn't move!

Large hands rested against her shoulders, gently but effectively holding her in place.

"Look at me, Sydney."

She had no choice but to do as he commanded. Still, she couldn't stop the quaking that gripped her body.

He nodded. "That's better. If you scream, the cop outside your door will throw me out of here."

What was he talking about? The hands moved away from her shoulders. Ironically, she wanted that reassuring contact back.

"Don't fade out on me, Sydney. Take a couple of deep breaths."

She licked at her chapped lips as she stared into his ruggedly handsome face. He wore a military dress uniform, she realized. Puzzling out why this should be significant was too hard for her muzzy brain to contemplate. It was enough that he was here. She relaxed, staring up at him, drawn to him in some indefinable way.

"Are you thirsty?" he asked.

Sydney nodded, bewildered, and suddenly, terribly tired. The last thing she remembered—

"No! Don't try to remember. Look at me, okay?"

Looking at him was the easiest thing she'd ever been asked to do. Just his presence made her feel safe and protected. He lifted a cup with a straw poking from the top. Carefully, he brought it to her lips in silent offering.

"Just a small sip," he cautioned.

The ice water slid down her grateful throat, soothing the strained, parched dryness. Her whole body felt strained. She hurt. Everywhere.

"Listen to me."

Dark somber eyes bored into her.

"Visiting hours don't start for some time yet, so I don't

know how long I'll have in here before one of the nurses comes to check on you.''

She blinked, trying to focus on those chiseled features. While he was somehow achingly familiar, she knew she'd never seen him before. How sad to have wasted all this time.

"You were shot during a bank robbery."

The muzzle of the gun. Deafening noise. Blood. So much blood.

Jerome!

"Easy. You're safe now," his voice continued.

Blood had pumped from Mrs. Argossy's fallen form to mingle with the spilled soda on the white tile floor.

"Listen to me, Sydney. You're safe."

His words banished the horrible images. His hand absently stroked her shoulder, calming the tremors that threatened to shake her apart.

"You're in the hospital. You've been here three days. Do you understand?"

She focused on his face, trying to still the living nightmare. His somber expression helped hold the horror at bay. Since it seemed important to him that she agree, she nodded.

"Who are you?" Her voice croaked, sounding as rusty and sore as it felt.

His lips thinned. "Noah."

The name took processing. "Jerome's brother?"

No. Anyone but Jerome's brother. Fate couldn't be so unkind. But that would explain the military uniform. Jerome had often talked about his brother, the major.

"Yes. I'm Jerome's brother."

Deep sadness filled his brooding expression. She wanted to reach out to him, to ease that sorrow. This was Jerome's brother!

Jerome.

She shut her eyes against the pain. In her head, the gunshots echoed, blending with the screams she'd locked inside. She smelled the sharp tang that had hung in the wisps of smoke. She felt Jerome's full weight crashing down on her as he stumbled forward and collapsed, his body jerking repeatedly, pinning her to the floor.

She didn't need the words, but her lips formed them anyhow. She opened her eyes. "He's dead," she stated. She knew it to be true.

"Yes."

Noah responded so softly she almost didn't hear him as the first salty tear trickled down her cheek.

"Don't," he said sharply. "Please. We need to talk before they toss me out of here."

She stared at him, frustrated by her inability to wipe the wetness from her cheek. "I wasn't planning to give in to hysterics."

His expression softened. "Good. That would send *me* screaming. Do you remember everything that happened?"

If only she could forget.

She tried to sit up and found she still couldn't move her hands. For the first time, she noticed the IV bottle on the other side of the bed. She blinked rapidly in frustration and Noah withdrew a crisp white handkerchief. He blotted her cheeks and eyes.

The elusive scent she'd noticed on awakening came from him, she realized. Probably a cologne, though it was so faint she couldn't be certain. The distracting smell helped to calm her, for some reason.

"Mrs. Argossy?"

"Dead," he answered quietly.

Sydney cringed.

"Take deep breaths," Noah encouraged.

A long shudder passed through her. Once again she tried to move. "My hands—"

"They tied you down so you wouldn't thrash around anymore. You pulled the IV out twice. They were afraid you'd injure yourself."

"What are you talking about?"

"You slammed your head against something when you fell, Sydney. You suffered a concussion. When you finally started to come to, you began to thrash around so violently that they had to sedate you."

"I don't remember." Yet she could almost remember horrible screams that felt lodged deep inside her. She stared up at him, focusing on his face in a bid for control. "My head hurts."

He nodded. "That's to be expected."

"*I* wasn't expecting it." He smiled and she relaxed. "Jerome didn't know you were coming, did he?"

Pain flashed in his dark eyes. "No. I was due for some leave next week, but I hadn't planned to come here."

Sydney didn't know what to say. She knew the brothers weren't close. And knowing her husband as well as she did now, she suspected more than age and distance had separated the men.

"Sydney, I know the timing is off, but we need to talk."

"I'm sorry, Noah. I'm afraid I'm muzzy. What—"

"So, you're awake at last! You aren't supposed to be in here at this hour, Mr. Inglewood. Official visiting hours don't start until ten."

The anemic-looking nurse bustled inside. She frowned at Noah, and came forward so she could stand officiously over the bed. "How are you feeling?"

Sydney didn't know how to answer the question. Mostly, she felt confused. Her gaze sought Noah. She sensed him willing her to remain in control and she swallowed hard.

"I'd like to move my hands," she managed.

"I'll check with the doctor. Do you know who you are?"

"Of course I know who I am."

The nurse waited.

"Sydney Edwards." She saw Noah's frown. "Inglewood," she added.

"Do you know where you are?"

"The hospital."

"Do you know why?"

Her irritation mounted along with her headache. Sydney glared at the nurse. "I was shot. Now, I'd like to speak to the doctor, please."

"He'll be by to see you shortly." The nurse planted a thermometer in her mouth.

Sydney thrust the offending object aside with her tongue. "Now!"

"Mrs. Inglewood, you really mustn't get excited."

Sydney stopped listening. "Will you get him for me?" she asked Noah, avoiding the thermometer.

He nodded. "I'll be back."

Sydney waited, but he didn't return. And by afternoon, she knew everything.

"I'm afraid we won't be able to determine if you'll regain the full use of all the fingers until after the swelling goes down," the self-important surgeon told her. "The nerve and muscle damage was extensive."

Staring at her completely bandaged right hand, Sydney was barely able to control the fearful anxiety the doctor's words created. Her career as a jeweler might be over. With only one usable hand, could she do the intricate work required? Her heart pounded. Her throat went dry.

Then he dropped his bombshell.

"Fortunately, the baby is fine. Your concussion had us worried at first, naturally, but it appears there's no permanent damage done there either. You may experience some headaches and a little dizziness from the concussion...."

Baby?

He might as well have spoken in Chinese.

"I'm pregnant?" Sydney could only stare at the man. Jerome's friend, the fertility doctor, had told them the procedure hadn't worked! "Are you certain?"

Thrown off stride by the interruption, the doctor rubbed the pen tip against the side of his face as if bewildered. "Quite certain, Mrs. Inglewood. You appear to be about three months pregnant. When was...?"

That incompetent twit! Hadn't she guessed she couldn't trust Jerome's friend? His entire clinic had done little to inspire confidence. She should have known he'd get the test results wrong.

"I got pregnant three months and nine days ago," she told the surgeon. That date was engraved on her mind for all time.

Like a delayed electric charge, the impact of his revelation suddenly slammed home. She was going to have a baby! Jerome's baby.

But Jerome was dead!

She'd been in the process of filing for a divorce.

She could not be pregnant! Not now! Not when this officious surgeon was implying that her hand might never function properly again and her whole career could be in jeopardy.

Panic clogged her throat while the surgeon stood beside her, calmly, arrogantly sure of himself as he continued to list her health concerns. The soft-spoken man hadn't a clue that his words were doing more to shock her than the bullet had done.

Sydney glanced at her stomach and shook her head in denial. She didn't look pregnant. She didn't feel pregnant. She did not want to be pregnant. Not now. She wanted this doctor to be wrong.

A vision of a tall man in a military uniform made her close her eyes in despair. Noah. She was pregnant with his brother's baby.

A shiver racked her entire body. This wasn't happening. She wanted to grab her pounding head and close her eyes until the nightmare ended.

"Mrs. Inglewood, I assure you," the surgeon continued, "the baby is fine. There's no cause for alarm."

Wanting to laugh, she also wanted to cry. No wonder she'd been thrashing around when she'd started to wake up. She wanted to thrash around again right now. Her entire world had just shifted one hundred eighty degrees.

She was relieved when the doctor finally left. Staring out the window, she tried to calm the insidious threat of panic welling in her chest. Pregnant! What was she going to do?

She hadn't liked the small fertility clinic or the hyper doctor who ran it, but Jerome had insisted on using both. The man was a former schoolmate. A friend. And his brand-new clinic needed patients. Small wonder. The creep also needed to go back to medical school.

Despite his assurance that the procedure hadn't worked, she was pregnant. She clutched the sheet covering her, wadding the material into a destructive ball. Whether the timing suited her or not, Sydney was going to have the child she'd always wanted.

The police and FBI arrived before she had time to think past the shock. Despite their effusive apologies for disturbing her, Sydney spent the bulk of the afternoon answering questions until her voice was hoarse and her head felt as if it were going to come apart in her hands.

The thieves had made off with more than three quarters of a million dollars. They hadn't left a trace of evidence behind. They'd even been smart enough to locate and take the bank's surveillance tapes. All the authorities had was Sydney, the only eyewitness to what had happened. Not that she was much help. Despite her best efforts, Sydney couldn't give them anything to work with. Exhausted, she fell asleep as soon as they left.

Dreams fragmented her sleep. Real events blended with menacing nightmares that brought her to the edge of waking. She knew she was dreaming, but she couldn't seem to force her heavy eyes open.

Fear became a writhing force in her chest as she faced the gunman all over again. In her dream, someone hovered just out of sight. The danger felt all too real. If only she could open her eyes to look.

Sydney struggled to release herself from the nightmare's hold. Her senses screamed at her to open her eyes. A crash pierced the nightmare, jarring her free. She opened her eyes and gasped for air. A bearded man with long hair stood beside her bed.

Piercing dark eyes glared down at her, plunging icy fear straight through her veins. He withdrew his hand from inside the nightstand drawer. Fingers flexed. A subtle threat. But there was no subtlety in the stare that drilled into her. The menace was real. She drew in a ragged breath of air to scream when a voice in the hall called out sharply.

"Hey, orderly! They need your help in 413! Someone fell!"

Without a word, the man turned and strode away.

Badly shaken, Sydney struggled to sit up. Pain clawed her head with needlelike talons. Dropping her chin to her chest, she pressed her palm against her throbbing temple, so dizzy she was nearly sick. The wave of vertigo passed, leaving her weak and spent in reaction. Only when she could finally open her eyes again and everything remained still did she notice the dinner tray sitting on the tray table beside her.

The drawer of her nightstand was partially open. A vase of flowers had fallen to the floor. It must have been the crash that had penetrated her nightmare.

Hand on the call button, she hesitated. Had the threat been real, or imagined? Had the orderly merely looked angry because he'd knocked over the vase and was afraid he'd be in trouble? Or was there another, more sinister reason?

Surely the police officer who'd summoned the man wouldn't have let anyone in her room without credentials.

But years of television cop shows said anyone could get a set of credentials. And she hadn't noticed any around his neck. Maybe he'd brought in her dinner tray and maybe he hadn't. For certain he'd knocked over the flowers. And his hands had been inside the drawer of her nightstand. He *could* have been searching for something to wipe up the mess, but the memory of his cold dark eyes sent her hand to the call light.

Minutes passed. No one came. Why wasn't anyone responding?

Shoving back the covers, Sydney stood. Dizzy, she grabbed the tray table for support. The stand began to roll.

''Mrs. Inglewood!''

A slip of a nurse rushed inside the room, barely in time to prevent her fall.

''I almost didn't catch you! Here sit down. There's

glass all over the floor! You knocked over a vase. You should have waited for someone to come and help you up. We had an emergency. The patient down the hall just fell out of bed. He's a large man and it took four of us to get him back in again. The last thing we need is for you to fall down, too. Do you need to go to the bathroom?''

"No!''

"Then what's the problem?''

"The man who was just in here, I think he brought this tray. Do you know him?''

Puzzled, the woman stared. "I don't know what man you're talking about. I didn't see who delivered the trays tonight. I'm not even the nurse for this section. I just saw your light flashing and…is there a problem?''

With the pretty young nurse looking up at her, Sydney started feeling foolish. What if she'd made a mistake? They would think she was some sort of paranoid fool. But if she hadn't made a mistake?

"Look, I know this sounds crazy, but I woke up and found him staring at me. Are you sure he really works here?''

The nurse started looking worried. "Did he say something inappropriate? Did he touch you?''

"No. No, he didn't do anything. I mean, besides knocking over that vase. But I don't think he was wearing identification. You know, like yours.''

The woman relaxed slightly, though she still looked concerned. "The police aren't letting anyone in here without identification, Mrs. Inglewood.''

"I know that! Please. Humor me. Just check him out, will you? Or have the police officer on duty check him out. Please!''

"All right. Tell me what the man looked like.''

"He had long brown hair and a beard and mustache. And piercing brown eyes."

The nurse relaxed. "Oh, him. Don't worry. He's the orderly that helped us get Mr. Logler off the floor. I think he's new, but I'll check just to make sure."

The loudspeaker came to life before Sydney could question that statement. "Karin Stipes, call in please."

"That's me. I swear there's a full moon out tonight. The whole place is going crazy. I'll be right back. And I'll check on that orderly for you. You just relax. You've been through quite an ordeal, from what I hear."

Sydney sank back against the pillows, feeling oddly unsettled. The nurse was placating her. She wanted to argue, but her head was killing her. If only Noah would return.

The thought surprised her. Why had she automatically thought of Noah? She didn't even know him, and that made her inutterably sad.

It must be the combination of the drugs in her system and the terrible nightmares that were throwing her thoughts into such chaos. She shouldn't be thinking of Noah at all.

No doubt she was simply overreacting to finding that orderly standing over her.

Sydney looked at the open drawer in her nightstand. Then she regarded the dinner tray.

And maybe she wasn't.

Despite the nurse's assurances, there had been something frightening about the orderly. If she was paranoid, so be it. Sydney wanted to go home.

Only, where was home? Certainly not the apartment she'd so briefly shared with Jerome. She couldn't go back there, any more than she could take back the things she'd said to him the last time they'd talked.

She had meant every word, but that only added to her guilt. Theirs had never been a normal marriage, but she'd gone into the situation with her eyes open—for the most part. Nothing could have prepared her for the changes in Jerome once they married. Yet, despite all their battles, she'd never wished him ill. They'd made a mistake. A mistake she'd been trying to rectify.

Whether by accident or design, she couldn't forget that Jerome had saved her life.

Sydney closed her eyes, turned her face into her pillow and gave in to the grief and fear suddenly crowding her mind. Sobs finally turned to hiccups, leaving her spent and listless. She must have fallen deeply asleep because she didn't see or hear whoever came in and took away her tray and cleaned up the broken vase of flowers.

Surprisingly, when she did wake, even her head felt better. Time passed slowly. Her eyes were closing again when someone entered the room. His scent reached her before she could turn her head to look in his direction. When she did, she had to battle another sudden wave of vertigo.

"You still look pretty bad," Noah said.

He was a tall, powerfully built man who carried himself with an air of assurance and authority that commanded attention. Alpha male, she thought. Used to being in charge. Yet instead of being repelled by this, she was curiously drawn to Noah.

He came to a halt beside her bed. Up close, she saw that circles pouched beneath Noah's eyes and lines of strain marred his strong features.

"Have *you* looked in a mirror recently?" she managed to respond, uncomfortably aware on a feminine level of how disheveled she must appear. It was crazy, this jolt of physical awareness she felt when he looked at her.

She wanted to ask him where he'd been. Why he hadn't come back as he promised earlier. Only she was afraid the questions would sound whiny. So she lifted her chin and met his gaze without flinching and tried to ignore the unsettling feelings deep inside.

Noah regarded her solemnly. He held an offering in his hand. A small African violet, she realized. She swallowed hard to keep unexpected tears at bay. What was happening to her emotions? Those tiny, velvety blue blossoms represented peace and contentment in her world. He couldn't have chosen anything better—or anything worse.

"Please. I want to go home."

She'd meant to thank him. The childish request came out instead. Noah set the plant on her nightstand.

"The doctor said maybe tomorrow."

She shook her head and immediately wished she hadn't. Stabbing pain lanced through her skull. Sydney gritted her teeth. "Now."

"You must be feeling better."

That didn't merit a response.

"Your friends are worried," he told her. "Hannah's new husband, Bruce, had a real battle to get her to leave on their honeymoon."

Astounded, she gaped at him. "I forgot all about the wedding!" She was to have been one of Hannah's bridesmaids. No wonder none of her friends had come by to see her.

Noah walked to the narrow window near her bed and looked out. "Hannah wanted to wait, but Laura and Bruce convinced her you would want her to go ahead with the ceremony."

Sydney nipped a trace of regret. She fervently wished she could have been there, but she was honestly glad Hannah hadn't postponed her wedding. Hannah and Bruce were so passionately in love that at times it was almost embarrassing.

"They tried to see you yesterday before the service," Noah continued, "but the police were with you. The doctor left instructions that you weren't to have visitors."

Sydney stared at him, appalled. "I would have seen them! No one told me they were here."

"No. I don't imagine they did." He pulled a heavy visitor's chair closer to the bed and sat down. He wasn't wearing his military uniform anymore, yet the formal white shirt and dark dress pants were practically a uniform when worn with such commanding elegance.

"You have loyal friends," he said slowly. "First, Hannah wanted to postpone the wedding, then she wanted to postpone the honeymoon."

"Oh. She didn't—"

"No, she didn't. She and Bruce left as scheduled."

Sydney relaxed. "How do you know them?"

"We spent a lot of time together in the waiting room. They even invited me to the wedding. I like your friends."

"So do I."

"Your friend, Laura, tried to cancel her flight out this morning, but she couldn't. She was going to try and make a last-minute swap. If she succeeds, she'll be by in the morning."

Laura was a flight attendant who'd complained long and hard about having to make a cross-country trip right after Hannah's wedding. Sydney remembered how they'd teased her about restricting her champagne intake. It felt like a lifetime ago. Now Hannah was married and Jerome was dead and nothing would ever be the same again.

"Easy," Noah said gently. He stared at her with unblinking eyes. Why did his presence seem to offer safety in a world gone mad? She had to stop thinking like that.

"I feel like I'm living in a nightmare. Tell me something, if I wasn't supposed to have visitors, how come they let you in?" she demanded, unsettled by her awareness of him. In truth, she suspected Noah hadn't waited for an invitation. Pesky things like hospital rules wouldn't stop him if he wanted something.

"I'm considered family."

Family. Her hand rested against her stomach. His eyes followed the motion and an intense look entered his features.

"We have to talk about this situation, Sydney."

He knew about the baby. It was there in his eyes. She thought of the new life growing inside her, of her tumultuous relationship with his brother and she tried not to let her sudden shudder show.

"Is everything all right?" His gaze fell to her abdomen. She resisted an impulse to touch her stomach again. She was oddly embarrassed by his knowledge of her condition.

"Everything's fine." Her entire world had just collapsed and been reformed, but everything was fine. Realizing she was about to give in to another bout of self-pity, Sydney sat up. "Would you find my clothing, please? I want to go home."

"We need to talk about the baby and your plans, Sydney."

"I want to get out of here," she repeated.

"Tomorrow."

"Tonight!"

His brow furrowed. "You need to think of the baby."

She closed her eyes against the pain that came from more than simply her throbbing head.

"Jerome's baby." As if she could think of anything else right now.

Noah's expression darkened. She couldn't think about him right now. Her head pounded with thoughts of the baby. She'd wanted a child badly enough to marry the wrong man just to have one. What a fool she'd been. Didn't they always say, be careful what you wish for?

Sydney pulled back the covers, ignoring Noah's frown, and started to swing her legs off the bed. He moved so quickly he startled her. His hand came down on her shoulder, kindly, but firmly. She couldn't meet his eyes. They saw entirely too much.

"I want my clothes."

"You don't have any clothes here, Sydney. They cut them off your body to check for injuries. You were covered in blood."

"Then I'll go home naked."

He half smiled. Her breath caught in her throat. Why, he was handsome. Nothing like Jerome, of course, but he would age with a depth and grace that would make him more striking with every year.

What was she thinking? She didn't care what Noah looked like. The man was her husband's brother!

"You won't have to go home naked," he was saying. "I'll stop by your apartment first thing in the morning and get you something to wear home."

"No!" She swallowed her instant panic and tried for a calm she was far from feeling. "I need to leave *now*."

All traces of humor disappeared from his face. He misunderstood her panic and regarded her steadily. "Are you always this bossy?"

"Yes." She couldn't bring herself to correct his impression. As soon as he saw the apartment she'd shared with his brother, he'd know how bad things had been between them. She wasn't ready to answer the sort of questions he would then ask. And he *would* demand explanations as soon as he realized how many of her belongings were gone from the apartment she'd supposedly shared with Jerome.

"You must have led Jerome around like a puppy."

The unfairness of his words stung. They couldn't have been farther from the truth. He knew nothing about her relationship with Jerome. And she wasn't about to tell him any details, either. She owed Jerome that much.

"The doctor said tomorrow morning," Noah temporized. "If you're well enough."

"I'm well enough right now." It was only a small lie. She felt weaker than a day-old kitten. A mangled, day-old kitten with a headache. But she could manage. She was used to managing.

Noah tipped his head to regard her. "My father told me I should never call a lady a liar."

"But you'll make an exception in my case?"

He ignored her challenge completely. "Morning is only a few hours away," he stated. "Get a good night's sleep and then we'll talk."

She thought of the nightmare and controlled another shudder.

"I'll make a few arrangements and bring you something to wear," he finished.

"What sort of arrangements?"

"You're going to need help."

She shook her head. The room spun slightly, forcing her eyes closed to combat the sensation. The doctor had said the vertigo would eventually go away. She should have asked him to define "eventually."

"I won't need any help," she told Noah. She kept her eyes shut to avoid looking up at him. "And if I do, that's my problem."

"And the baby?"

"Jerome is dead. The baby is my problem as well."

She would never allow another man in her life who thought he could tell her what to do or how to do it.

"I'd like to help."

That snapped her eyes open. "Why?"

His eyes flared with a tumble of emotions. He started to respond and stopped. Sydney realized she was rubbing her temples to try and ease the pounding pain in her head and dropped her hands to the sheet. Noah walked to the window. Silence stretched between them.

"Sydney, I signed the papers to have my only brother buried yesterday morning," Noah said suddenly. "There was nothing I could do to help him. Won't you at least let me try to help you?"

His words shocked her anew. "You already had Jerome buried?"

"Yes. We'll hold a memorial service for him when you're well enough."

"You had no right!"

Noah turned back to her, sadness etched in the creases about his eyes. His expression was filled with regret and compassion. "I guess not. I'm sorry, Sydney."

She couldn't stand the pain in Noah's expression. The truth was, he did have rights. Probably more than she had. His remorse disturbed her almost as much as the chaos of her thoughts. Noah wasn't to blame for anything. He was doing his best to help, yet she was snapping at him like a rabid dog.

"Why didn't you wait?" she asked more calmly.

"The morgue released the body. I had decisions to make—so I made them."

His small shrug tugged at her heart. Despite his size and self-assurance, Noah was a vulnerable man.

"Your concussion had the doctors worried," he continued. "You kept slipping in and out of consciousness. They didn't know how soon you'd be able to make decisions."

"It's okay. I understand." And she did. She would have made the same arrangements if she'd been able to. She settled back against the bed, suddenly exhausted.

He rested his hand lightly on her arm. "Thank you."

"No. I'm the one who should be thanking you. For the plant and…for everything else." His touch disturbed her.

Who was she trying to kid? Everything about him disturbed her. He was a kind, caring sort of man.

He was also Jerome's brother.

"Did you know Jerome saved my life?" she asked, wanting to erase some of the hurt he must be feeling.

"The investigators told me." A muscle, clenched too tightly, twitched in Noah's stern jaw. "He must have loved you very much."

Oh, God. The truth lay bitterly in her mind. Could Noah read that truth in her eyes? She closed them against his invasive stare.

"I'd like to take care of you, Sydney. At least make sure you and the baby are settled and have everything you need."

She turned away and shoved a hand through her hair. Noah was Jerome's brother, but he was also a stranger. She'd learned a long time ago that the only one she could depend on was herself. "I appreciate the offer, but—"

He stopped her words with an outstretched palm. "Please. Just stay here and rest until morning like the doctor ordered. Then I'll see about getting you sprung. When you're feeling stronger, you can tell me to go if that's what you want. In the meantime—"

"And will you?" Or would he be like Jerome, turning

possessive, demanding, insistent that things had to be his way or no way?

Noah's lips gave a wry twist. "Will I go? Well, maybe not right away, but I'd rather have this battle when you don't look like a puff of wind could blow you over. If you'll give me the keys to your apartment..."

Sydney pointed at the nightstand as lethargy settled over her. Sooner or later he was going to learn the truth. Did it really make any difference if he went to the apartment now?

Noah reached into the drawer next to her bed and withdrew her purse. Sydney found her gaze riveted on the dark stains that marred the white leather surface. As he fished out her keys, images flashed before her eyes. Soda and blood. The bank enclosure had run with both.

She slumped back against the pillow. Bile rose in her throat.

"Hey. What is it? Are you feeling sick? Should I call for the nurse?"

"No." She choked out the word and shut her eyes. "Could you...would you take the purse away with you?"

Her blood, Mrs. Argossy's or Jerome's? Did it matter? She never wanted to see that handbag again.

Without a word, he emptied the contents into the open drawer. "I'll bring you another purse tomorrow. Is there a particular outfit you'd like?" he asked.

Sydney shook her head.

Once again, his hand rested lightly on her shoulder. The gesture offered both friendship and concern.

"Get some rest tonight. I'll be back in the morning."

"I'm not your responsibility." She had to say it even though part of her was selfishly glad he cared. She was so tired of always being strong.

"I know. I'll be back. Call if you need anything. I left the hotel number under your telephone."

"Thank you."

She watched him disappear through the doorway and reaffirmed the decision she'd made when she'd faced the investigators. Jerome was the father of her baby. The man who had saved her life. He'd been Noah's only family, and in the eyes of the world, Jerome had died a hero.

No one would ever learn what she suspected.

THEY WOKE HER again to give her a sleeping pill. She couldn't believe they actually did that. Groggily, she accepted the pill, put it in her mouth and swallowed the water. As soon as the nurse left, Sydney spit the pill out. She didn't need drugs that would make her fuzzy. She needed a clear head in the morning so they'd let her go home. She rolled over and went back to sleep.

It could have been minutes or hours later when she roused from another disturbing cycle of dreams. Her heart was beating much too fast and her breath came in short pants. She struggled to focus on yet another person entering her room. How was she supposed to get any rest when they kept waking her every time she fell asleep?

Darkness shadowed the room. Restlessly, she watched the person close the door to the hallway without a sound. The empty bed next to hers took on a ghostly appearance in the dim light filtering in through the solitary window. Maybe that was why the figure's approach appeared almost stealthy.

Sydney's heart began thumping more quickly.

The person was too silent. He'd closed the door. A nurse who'd come to check on her wouldn't close the door. Instantly, she pictured the bearded orderly.

Slowly, she inched her fingers toward the call light,

afraid to let him know she was awake. The impression of danger grew stronger as the person neared the bed. There was something wrong with his face. Her vision shouldn't be blurry. She hadn't swallowed the sleeping pill. Yet she couldn't make out any features.

Her fingers found the call button. Sydney pressed it as the man suddenly rushed forward, knocking the button from her hand.

Sydney screamed. A rubber-glove-encased hand clamped over her mouth, choking off the sound. The other hand circled her throat in a breath-stealing grip.

In that instant, she realized he wore a ski mask over his head.

Desperately, she threw herself to one side. Pain radiated down her arm as her bandaged hand struck the bed rail.

"Where is it?"

The waft of garlic was sickening. She clawed at those short, blunt fingers pressing into her throat. He was incredibly strong. She couldn't breathe!

She beat at his face while his voice continued to demand. Didn't he realize she couldn't answer? If she could just reach his eyes!

Blackness dimmed her vision. Her head swam with vertigo.

Noah had been wrong. Following the doctor's orders had been a terrible idea. In fact, it was about to get her killed.

Chapter Two

The telephone pulled him out of a restless sleep. Noah glanced at the clock and saw it was only 5:56 in the morning. He sat up, tensing as he reached for the phone. He fully expected the message to be a call to duty. Instead, a prissy feminine voice filled his ear.

"Major Inglewood? This is Jennifer Comsilt. I'm a nursing supervisor at—"

"Sydney?"

"She's going to be all right," the professional voice hastened to assure him. "However, she did indicate that she would like me to call you."

Fully alert, Noah swung his legs over the side of the bed. "She indicated? She didn't ask?"

"Her...ah...that is, there was an incident early this morning."

He was reaching for his pants, the receiver tucked under his chin. "What sort of incident, Ms. Comsilt?"

Was she okay? The baby!

Noah sorted through the horrible possibilities running through his head while fear feasted on his stomach. He dressed rapidly, by rote.

"Let me reiterate," the woman's voice continued, "Mrs. Inglewood will be fine, but...well, someone entered her room sometime after four o'clock this morning and...that is, they attempted...to strangle her.''

Coldness seeped into his chest. She'd wanted to leave and he'd left her there. ''I'm on my way.''

''That isn't—''

Noah disconnected. The woman had said Sydney was all right but he needed to see for himself.

He dug through his duffel bag and pulled out the only items of clothing he had that might work for her. Bundling them together, he reached for his key card, stuffed his feet into his shoes and was out the door and into the early-morning heat of what would no doubt prove to be another humid summer day in Washington, D.C. His hotel was only a ten-minute drive from the hospital, yet the cab ride seemed interminable.

He kept remembering that Sydney hadn't wanted to stay. He should have listened to her. How had the attacker gotten inside her room? What had happened to the armed officer stationed outside her door?

Less than twenty minutes after the phone call woke him, Noah was stepping off the elevator onto Sydney's floor. People milled about the nurses' station. Coffee and breakfast scents mingled with the normal hospital smells. Carts bearing breakfast trays were being rolled along at the far end of the hall.

A different uniformed police officer now stood, rather than sat, outside the door to Sydney's room. A second plainclothes officer was positioned at the desk, talking with an agitated nurse. An assortment of other people clustered around. Noah recognized the FBI agent as soon as the man turned in his direction.

''Major Inglewood? I'm Agent Wickowski. We met—''

"I remember. You're FBI, investigating the bank robbery."

"That's correct. The police called me this morning to tell me what had transpired."

"What exactly *did* transpire, Agent Wickowski?"

The man hurried to catch up as Noah strode toward Sydney's door without waiting for an answer. "Major—"

"How did anyone get past the police officer?"

A flush crept up his neck. "There was a miscommunication between our office and the police department. Apparently it was...er...necessary to pull the officer last night. The police felt since we'd already taken her statement..."

Noah eyed him coldly, stopping the words in the man's throat. "She's the only eyewitness to what happened."

"Yes, but her whereabouts weren't reported. They didn't think—"

"Obviously."

The uniformed officer stepped forward to block the door at Noah's approach.

"Do I go through him, or around him?" Noah asked mildly.

The agent inclined his head and the uniformed man stepped away with a tight look. Noah would have welcomed a scuffle, if only to work off some of the tension humming through his body.

Sydney perched on the edge of the bed, the shapeless hospital gown drooping off one shoulder. Her hair hung in lank strands past her shoulders, surrounding a face pale enough for Halloween. Her china-blue eyes were large as saucers. But she appeared extraordinarily calm for someone who'd just been attacked. Her expression brightened instantly when she saw him.

"Sorry, Sydney," he told her without preamble. "Are you okay?"

She gave a small nod. He noted the new bruises and his jaw set.

"Want to leave?"

In answer, she tried to scoot off the bed. He caught her before she pitched forward, tangled in the sheet. "Easy. I've got you."

His arm came to rest across her chest, supporting the lush curve of one breast. Sydney was a tall, shapely woman. How shapely, he shouldn't be noticing.

"Okay?"

She nodded.

"You're not thinking of taking her out of here?" Wickowski demanded.

"Thinking, no. I *am* taking her out of here."

"Look, Major—"

"No, Wickowski, you look. She was almost killed. I assume the guy wasn't caught?"

His ruddy cheeks grew ruddier.

Sydney laid a hand against Noah's chest. "Please." Her voice was low and hoarse. "Fight later. I'd like to leave now."

"Right away," he agreed.

"I could hold her as a material witness," Wickowski threatened.

"You can try." Noah met the agent's anger with his own. They'd nearly let her be killed!

Wickowski looked away first.

More people crowded into the room, blocking their path to the door. A rotund, pinch-faced woman with faded red hair stepped forward importantly. "Major Inglewood, I'm Jennifer Comsilt. We spoke on the telephone. *This* is Dr. Messinger."

Jennifer Comsilt pushed at a prim pair of glasses sitting on her nose while the doctor fussed with a stethoscope hanging around his neck. Noah dismissed them with a glance.

"I'd like to use the bathroom," Sydney whispered.

"You want to help her, Ms. Comsilt?"

"Oh." The supervisor gazed frantically past him as if looking for someone else. "Er…ah, yes. Of course." Obviously, she wasn't used to making personal contact with the patients.

"I can manage," Sydney told him.

He gave her shoulder a gentle squeeze. "I don't doubt it for a minute, but I think getting dressed will be easier with some help, don't you? Here." He thrust the bundle of clothing into Mrs. Comsilt's free hand. "These won't be a great fit, but they're the best I could come up with on such short notice."

"Not mine?" Sydney asked in a whispery voice.

"Mine, I'm afraid. I didn't get to your place last night."

She paused, surveying him from head to toe. A spark of amusement glinted in her eyes. "Should be a great fit."

Noah found himself smiling wryly. "The jogging shorts have a drawstring," he offered.

"Uh-huh."

"Don't worry. The T-shirt will probably cover them completely."

"No doubt."

Her easy acceptance surprised him. He expected Sydney to be weak and needy. Her unexpected grit kept amazing him.

Messinger stepped forward. "Just a moment. Mrs. Inglewood suffered a trauma to her throat this morning." Messinger's grating voice had a nasal whine. "While I don't believe any permanent harm was done, I'd like a specialist to have a look at her.''

"I'll see to it. We're leaving in five minutes. You want to get the release forms?''

"Mr. Inglewood, this hospital cannot be responsible—''

"Save it, Doctor. I am *not* in the mood. We'll need the release papers right away or we're leaving without signing them.''

"Major Inglewood,'' the agent tried to cut in.

Noah spun toward the man. "Wickowski, my brother is dead. My sister-in-law just came too close to joining him for my peace of mind. She's...''

"We'll keep someone at her door.''

"...getting out of here right now. You've got her statement. Two days' worth, as a matter of fact.''

"I realize that. But in an investigation like this one, questions come up. The FBI—''

"Doesn't have to talk to her here in the hospital. Cut her some slack, Wickowski. I'm taking her someplace safe.''

"Police protection—''

"Isn't very reliable, wouldn't you say?''

The doctor interrupted. "Mrs. Inglewood is pregnant!'' he protested.

The last thing Noah needed was a reminder of the child growing inside his brother's wife. He'd thought about little else since he learned that fact. The ramifications were staggering. He leveled his coldest gaze on the man.

"I am aware of that, Doctor,'' he said with such quiet steel that anyone who knew him would have beaten a hasty retreat. "And I'm going to see that she lives to deliver that child. Three minutes, Doctor.''

The bathroom door opened. While no doubt the drawstring on the shorts had been cinched around her narrow waist as tightly as possible, the material hung in ridiculous fashion against long, shapely legs. The baggy T-shirt draped over the full swell of her generous breasts, making it all too obvious Sydney wasn't wearing a bra beneath the thin cotton. Noah decided he'd deck the first man who ogled her.

Sydney leaned on the nurse, but she straightened the moment she saw him. In that unguarded moment, he glimpsed a vulnerability that arced straight for his gut. She was shaken to the core and doing everything she knew to keep it from showing.

"Sydney, Agent Wickowski is offering you police protection."

"No!"

"Mrs. Inglewood, this time we'll use our own people. I promise you we'll see that you're protected."

"Am I under arrest?"

Her voice was stronger, though it still had a hoarse, raspy edge.

Wickowski shook his head. "Of course not."

"Then I'd like to leave."

"That's it, Wickowski. We're out of here." Noah's own instincts clamored for him to get her away as quickly as possible.

"Mrs. Inglewood," the doctor interjected, "this isn't a good idea. You've suffered a severe trauma to your head and you've just had surgery on your hand. You're taking a big risk leaving here."

"Bigger risk...staying," she croaked out as her voice broke down in a hoarse whisper.

"Don't strain your vocal cords," Noah chastised, reaching inside her closet for the bag of torn, stained clothing. "We're leaving."

He liked the way she stood up to the doctor. She was no cringing wimp, that was for sure. He went back to her drawer and collected the contents of her purse.

Sydney got discharge papers and lectures, but Noah had her in a wheelchair and out front before her breakfast tray arrived.

"Impressive," Sydney whispered. "I can see why you're a major."

In one hand, she clutched the African violet. He felt ridiculously pleased. She'd left behind the large sprays of flowers from her friends and co-workers.

Long sooty lashes fluttered closed when she leaned back against the cab's upholstery. Noah resisted an urge to smooth away the dark smudges of fatigue beneath the fall of lashes. He had to keep reminding himself that this was his brother's wife.

Staring at her profile, he decided Jerome's photographs hadn't done her justice. Sydney Edwards Inglewood had flawless skin over the sort of bone structure that gave her a clean, natural beauty.

"Thank you for getting me out of there."

"I should have listened to you last night. I didn't know they were going to pull the guard at your door."

Her shoulders lifted and fell in a small shrug. "They didn't know I was in danger."

"You'd think they'd protect a material witness better than that. Can you tell me what happened without straining your voice?"

In a husky whisper, Sydney told him what little she'd seen. "He wanted something, but he was so afraid I'd scream again he kept holding on to my throat so I couldn't answer even if I'd wanted to. I wonder if it could have been that orderly who scared me earlier."

"What orderly?"

Sydney's explanation fed his anger.

"You mean to tell me that no one checked this out?"

Sydney shrugged. "The nurse never came back. Or if she did, I was already asleep. Maybe the orderly was just weird, but in retrospect, I think he was going through the drawer on the nightstand."

Noah was coldly furious. "Is anything missing?"

"I never looked."

"We'll do that when we get to the hotel."

"I didn't have anything worth taking, Noah. Maybe ten dollars and some change. And I could be wrong about what he was doing."

"Did you tell Wickowski about this?"

She shook her head.

"We'll call him later."

He helped her from the cab in front of his hotel and she stumbled over the curb, forcing him to reach for her.

"Lean on me," he told her quietly. "We don't need you falling down in front of half the visiting businessmen in the city."

Men and women in power suits, sporting briefcases and newspapers, moved busily about the lobby. There were even a few early-morning tourists scurrying about.

Sydney stiffened. "I won't fall."

"Good. I hate scenes first thing in the morning."

"Then move your hand or you're going to get a doozy."

He realized that in avoiding her bad arm, his hand had pressed against the soft round curve of her breast. Instantly, he released her. Sydney moved forward with quiet dignity.

"Why are we here?"

"This is where I'm staying." He reached for the elevator button.

She raised her eyebrows expressively.

"I didn't think you wanted to answer any more questions for a while."

After a second she gave a delicate shudder and looked away. "I don't."

As a crush of people jostled their way out of the elevator, Sydney was pressed up against him. He steadied her lightly, careful of his hands this time. But that only reinforced his awareness of her body. A very nice body. She was a good height for a woman, almost at eye level with him.

The sudden flare of awareness in her eyes caught him off guard. Her lips parted. A lacy sweep of pink brightened her cheeks. His answering response came as another surprise. As soon as they entered the elevator away from prying eyes, he stepped away from her.

"My room has two double beds, Sydney," he said to reassure her as well as himself. "You can use the second one to try for a little sleep while I make other arrangements."

She wouldn't meet his eyes. "Who put you—?"

"In charge? I did." Her whispery voice only added fuel to the unwanted kindling of awareness. "You'd better stop trying to talk. You're losing what little voice you have left."

Her eyes narrowed and she lifted her head. "I realize you haven't seen any proof of this so far, but I am quite capable of taking care of myself, Major." Her voice dropped even lower as it cracked and broke. "I've been doing so for a number of years."

"I know. Jerome told me you were an orphan."

It had only confirmed his conviction that Jerome was a fool who'd let himself be trapped by a needy older woman with a biological clock ticking away.

On the other hand, Jerome had always liked to get his own way, so Noah figured it was the woman who would come to regret the decision. Jerome was a handsome charmer. He was also totally self-centered and used to being catered to.

Still, Noah had found himself studying Sydney's photograph at odd moments, baffled by the woman Jerome had selected for his wife. While pretty, she wasn't the flashy adornment Noah had expected Jerome to pick.

"I'm sorry I didn't make your wedding," Noah told her. "I was out of the country at the time."

"He would have liked you to be there," she said without looking at him.

Privately, Noah doubted that.

"It was a simple service. We didn't even use a church."

Was that a trace of regret? Noah couldn't tell. The last assignment had left Noah taking a hard look at the choices he'd made in his own life. He'd experienced a tug of envy over the life his brother had planned. Talk about irony. Noah risked his life every time he went on a mission, yet it was Jerome who'd died protecting someone else, leaving Noah the living hostages to fortune.

Noah was relieved when the elevator doors opened and he could abandon that train of thought. He led Sydney down the hall.

"How did you come to be an orphan?" he asked abruptly, curious about the woman his brother had married.

"My parents and older brothers were killed in an avalanche on a skiing vacation in Austria when I was seven."

"That's rough."

Remembered grief reflected in her eyes. "I was supposed to go with them, but I came down with chicken pox the day before the trip so I stayed with my grandmother.''

''So you weren't a total orphan?''

With an impatient toss of her hair she shook her head. ''She died of a massive heart attack when I was sixteen. Do you really want my life history?''

He unlocked the door to his room. ''Maybe later. Does it bother you to talk about the past?''

''No.''

He gestured her inside the room and she entered cautiously, almost as if she expected someone to jump out at her.

''Have a seat,'' he said brusquely.

''You must scare the heck out of young recruits.''

''What do you mean?''

''You're good at giving orders and intimidating people.''

He found himself wanting to smile again. ''I don't scare you.''

She arched her eyebrows again. ''Remember that.''

He suppressed an urge to chuckle. He hadn't expected to like Sydney so much. He laid a finger over her cracked lips. ''Save your voice. You can yell at me later. Right now you look done in.''

She studied him through eyes semiglazed by pain and fatigue. He sensed both grief and fear hiding beneath the surface and held up a hand to stave off any further protests. ''I'll try to stop giving orders. In the meantime, let's not argue until you're back to fighting form. Do you want to eat or sleep first? You'll be safe here, Sydney.''

Her eyes spoke volumes, but she turned without a word and set the plant on the nightstand. She moved stiffly to the far bed with its undisturbed cover.

"It's silly, but I'm so tired I can't even think straight anymore," she murmured.

"It's not silly at all." He stripped down the covers and let her climb into bed, still clothed in his running outfit. Sydney wasn't the sort to lean on anyone if she could help it. That she let him help her and didn't even protest when he smoothed the blanket over her told him a great deal about how bad she was feeling. He'd been right not to initiate a serious discussion right away. There'd be time later.

He'd meant to keep his actions strictly impersonal, but as her eyes fluttered closed, his hand reached out and gently stroked the hair back from her face. She twitched, but that was all. He would have sworn she was asleep in seconds.

Noah sat at the table and watched the steady rise and fall of her breathing and tried to control the unexpected spike from his libido. Sydney would be shocked if she knew the sort of urges she was stirring in him. He was feeling a little shocked himself.

No other woman had provoked this raw need to protect and cherish. Why Sydney of all people? Unless it had something to do with the baby she carried. He'd shied away from thoughts of the child ever since she'd uttered those damning words. *Jerome's baby.*

He ran unsteady fingers through his hair. What a mess. His brain knew she was his brother's wife, but his body didn't seem to care.

He stared at her hand, lying protectively curled across her chin. She had long, graceful fingers and short, unpolished nails, but it was her ring finger that captured his attention. She wore a simple, wide gold wedding band and an ordinary diamond solitaire on her left hand.

Glad to have a focus—any focus that would keep him

from looking at her—he studied her ring. She designed jewelry for a living. He would have expected something different on her finger—something unique. Obviously, he would have been wrong. Still, that jarring note was one more in a growing list of inconsistencies he'd noticed since he arrived.

Finally convinced that it would take the entire Army marching band to wake her, Noah made a couple of phone calls to get his mind off the bewitching woman. The last one was to Agent Wickowski, who expressed anger at not being told about the orderly. He wanted to come over and talk with Sydney right away. Noah convinced him to wait and suggested Wickowski talk with the nurse and the police officer first.

For a long time after that, Noah watched Sydney sleep, sorting through his options. He didn't have many, he acknowledged glumly. He couldn't simply walk away from her or the situation. He and Jerome had a blood tie he couldn't deny. And now Noah was irrevocably bound to Sydney. The thought was nearly as disturbing as the woman herself.

She looked almost ethereal in sleep. How would she look when she grew round with the baby she carried?

Following that line of thought would lead to disaster, Noah told himself. Impatiently, he stood and put out the Do Not Disturb sign. Then he called the desk to ask them to hold all calls. Disgruntled, he lay down on the other bed and willed himself back to sleep. Questions loomed in his mind. He tried to picture Sydney and Jerome together and the image made him angry and restless.

When she sat up hours later, he was still awake, still trying to figure out how to initiate the discussion they needed to have.

She rolled over and looked at him, her eyes misty with sleep. "Hi."

"Feel better?"

"I think so. Why are we whispering?"

"So we don't strain your voice?"

"Oh." She moistened her dry lips. "What have you been doing?"

"Watching you sleep."

She blinked in surprise. "You do lead an eventful life, don't you?" and she yawned, stretching away the kinks.

Noah's attention riveted on the material of the T-shirt where it tightened over the gentle swell of her breasts. She caught him looking and color suffused her face.

Heat stole up his neck as well. When was the last time he'd been caught staring at a woman like some randy schoolboy?

Sydney rolled off the other side of the bed before he could apologize. "Bathroom," she whispered without looking at him.

Well, at least she was steadier on her feet now. Noah sat up, frowning when the shower started.

She was too weak and dizzy. She could fall, hit her head. Anything might happen. Bathrooms were dangerous places. There was also the cast on her hand to consider. He didn't know if she was supposed to get it wet or not but it would definitely hamper her in the bathtub.

Noah suspected it wouldn't do him much good to point out either of those facts to her. Sydney Edwards—Inglewood, he tacked on sternly—definitely had a mind of her own.

Running a hand through his hair, he decided it would be much better for both of them if he didn't dwell on the image of her standing on the other side of that flimsy door taking a shower.

"I needed a nap more than she did," he muttered to himself as he reached for the telephone to call room service.

Sydney stepped from the steamy bathroom a few minutes later, a towel wrapped loosely around her head. She'd donned his T-shirt again, but the shorts had obviously proved too much for her. She gripped the drooping shorts firmly around her waist. He wished she looked ridiculous—instead of sexy as hell.

"Quite a fashion statement," he told her with what he hoped was an easy smile.

She looked down at the shirt where it clung a bit damply to the tops of her breasts and made a face. "I couldn't retie the drawstring with only one hand." Her embarrassment was tempered by annoyance.

Noah forced his eyes up and away, disturbed by his instant reaction. "I should have thought of that. I'll help you."

He could be detached. Of course he could.

"Come here."

Sydney hesitated.

Remembering her earlier comment about the way he gave orders he added, "Please."

Her expression lightened in a sudden burst of humor. "I'll bet that didn't hurt a bit."

"What didn't?"

"Saying please."

"Anybody ever tell you that you have a sassy mouth?"

She grinned. "No one dares. Have you been in the military a long time?"

She was stalling. He didn't mind the delaying tactics a bit. Touching her so intimately was going to be uncomfortable for both of them, especially since he knew she wasn't wearing a thing under those bits of cloth.

"I got a military scholarship in high school."

"ROTC?"

He nodded and perched on the edge of the bed so he could reach for the string.

"You know, we could call the front desk," she said suddenly, backing up. "They might have a gift shop. Maybe I could have them send up a dress or something."

He could just envision trying to help her into a dress. "I don't think so, but picking up your clothing will be our first priority." His sanity might depend on it. "Come here."

With an air of resignation, she approached. "I feel like a little kid," she said with endearing nervousness.

"Trust me, you don't look anything at all like a kid." And that was a pity. He wouldn't have thought twice about helping a kid.

He'd never felt such intense physical awareness of a woman before. He had to keep telling himself she was his brother's wife. Surely he could do this without embarrassing both of them.

But sitting on the bed had been a mistake. It put him just above eye level of the rounded curves his T-shirt strove to conceal. Her nipples contracted into tiny hard points. Noah tried not to stare and reminded himself once more that this was his sister-in-law, not some woman he was trying to take to bed.

"Sorry," she said. "I feel foolish."

He knew the feeling.

"Is this the spot where I'm supposed to close my eyes and think of God and country?"

She surprised a chuckle out of him. He liked the way she turned to humor in difficult situations. "I thought it was queen and country."

"Only if you're British."

"Ah. Well, c'mere darlin'," he said with a drawl.

Her expression flashed with mild alarm that immediately turned to an answering grin. "Go for it, Tex."

She released her one-hand death grip on the scrunched-up shirt and lost her hold on the jogging shorts underneath. They slid dangerously down her slim hips.

"Oops!"

Noah stopped their descent at her hips, which placed his face only inches from her navel beneath the thin bit of cotton. He inhaled the pleasant scent of the soap she'd used all over her body.

This had been a very bad idea.

"Here," he said a bit gruffly. "You hold the shorts. I'll get the drawstring."

Their hands connected. Noah drew in a sharp breath and reminded himself once more that this was his sister-in-law. Calling on every bit of discipline he'd ever known, he tugged up the hem of the T-shirt and reached for her waistband.

"I think I'd better tell you that I'm ticklish."

Noah stopped, his fingers barely touching her smooth marble skin. "Ticklish?"

"Very ticklish. And I always get even."

"Then it's a good thing I'm not ticklish."

"There are better ways of getting even."

"I think I like the sound of that." He slid a finger beneath the edge of the waistband searching for the drawstring. He tried not to acknowledge the silky feel of her skin as he brushed against the indentation that was her belly button. Her tummy contracted in instant reaction to his touch. His groin tightened in answer.

"Noah…"

"Don't move. Don't even breathe," he warned.

He tugged the drawstring loose, tied it and sat back, breathing as though he'd just run a marathon.

Sydney jumped back like a scalded cat. The towel on her head tilted to one side and she pulled it free.

"Well. Now. That wasn't so bad."

"Speak for yourself," he muttered under his breath.

"Thank you."

"Don't mention it."

He stood and walked to his duffel bag so she wouldn't notice the effect that little encounter had had on him. He needn't have worried. Sydney was looking everywhere but at him. He pulled items randomly from his kit.

"I need to borrow your comb, if you don't mind."

"Use anything you need."

Just don't tell me about it, he almost added. The intimacy of this situation was taking a high toll on his good intentions. "I'm going to grab a quick shower myself. If room service comes before I'm done, check the peephole before you open the door. If you aren't certain, wait for me. Okay?"

Her eyebrows raised mockingly. "Were you a drill instructor by any chance?"

He managed a lopsided smile, relieved she'd found a way to cut the tension between them. "Sorry again. I'm used to giving orders."

"I can tell."

"I just don't want you to take any chances."

"Yes, sir, Major, sir. Go take your shower."

Sydney watched him go with a mixture of relief and regret. Her reaction to that little scene had been juvenile, to say the least. She tried to tell herself that there had been nothing sensual in Noah's touch except in her own warped mind, but the truth was, for a minute or two there, they'd been a man and a woman who were attracted to each other. She didn't want to know what he must be thinking of her.

Noah was much nicer than she'd expected from the things Jerome had told her. Oh, Noah could be every bit as bossy as his much younger brother, but he took her refusal to obey in stride.

Noah wasn't Jerome. He'd gone out of his way to put her at ease despite his dominating tendencies. And if she could still feel the touch of his fingers against her bare skin, well, she'd just have to find ways to become more independent while her hand was in a cast—especially when it came to the awkward process of getting dressed.

Most of her belongings were at Laura's apartment and that was going to require an explanation. Noah was bound to think it odd that she and Jerome had separate bedrooms. She should just tell him the truth and be done with it, but she was embarrassed. She didn't want to see disdain in Noah's expression. Or pity. Jerome had been his brother. What would Noah think when he discovered their marriage had been a total sham from the start?

Her gaze fell on the deep blue African violet. She thought of the plant stand in her bedroom where a dozen more violets sat beneath the window. She'd planned to move them all to Laura's place this week.

She ran her finger gently over a soft round leaf. Noah couldn't possibly know how much she loved the delicate plants. Unless he'd already been inside the apartment. Or Jerome had told him. The brothers had been doing a lot of talking in recent months. Jerome was excited by that fact.

In fact, Noah had called during her final battle with Jerome. While the two were on the phone, she'd packed her bags and left the apartment. The decision hadn't been easy. She wasn't a quitter by nature, but she also wasn't going to become a victim in a relationship that was becoming more and more turbulent.

She and Jerome had married because they seemed to like each other and wanted to raise a family. It had been that simple and that complicated. She'd accepted that they would never have a normal physical relationship. She'd thought having a child was all that mattered. She thought of her reaction to Noah and shook her head. It was hard to believe her sheer stupidity.

Sydney stared at the rings on her finger. How had it come to this? She hated knowing Jerome had died while bitter words lay between them. And her guilt was compounded by her bizarre attraction to Noah.

Her gaze slid to the bathroom door. Noah had left it slightly ajar, probably so he'd hear her if she called out. She was touched by his unexpected kindness, yet disturbed by the way her body responded to him. She wasn't sure how to act around this stranger who was suddenly her self-proclaimed protector.

The scent she'd come to associate with Noah wafted out on wisps of steam. It amazed her to realize that, despite her mix of feelings, she felt safe with Noah.

When he finally stepped into the room, her gaze was instantly drawn to his broad chest, still damp from his shower. She drew in a breath as he pulled on a crisp white shirt, completely at ease with himself, and thankfully unaware of the jittery effect the sight of his bare chest had on her pulses.

Sydney jumped as someone rapped sharply on the door.

"It's okay," Noah said soothingly. "That will be the food. Stay there. I'll get it."

He returned with a wheeled cart and she sniffed appreciatively as he set out the meal. She would have preferred to do her own ordering, but she was too hungry to argue.

She did, however, eye the pot of tea in surprise.

"Not coffee?"

"My mother believed tea was a cure-all," he explained. "When I was a kid, tea appeared every time I had a sniffle. I made out okay so I figured it couldn't hurt in case your throat was still sore."

She pulled the tea bag from the water. "I thought chicken soup was supposed to be the cure-all."

When he turned that full smile on her, she forgot all the reasons she should be wary of Noah. The planes of his face softened into a devastatingly potent charm that was far more captivating than blatant good looks.

"I've heard that myth too," he agreed.

When Noah smiled like that a woman better be heavily grounded in reality, Sydney decided, or she'd find herself in a helpless puddle at his feet.

"You know, I've been thinking about the attacker," she told Noah after a time, breaking their comfortable silence and shoving the remains of her lunch to one side. "I don't think the attacker meant to choke me like that. I think he was trying to keep me from screaming and applied too much pressure. But I wish I knew what it was he wanted from me."

Noah reached out and stroked her arm. He had rough, coarse hands with strangely long, graceful fingers. There was strength in those hands.

"You showed amazing presence of mind pressing that call button, Syd. That action probably saved your life."

"You know, I hate being called Syd."

He smiled, another slow smile she felt clear to her toes.

"I'll try to remember that. What do you say we go over to your apartment and get you something to wear?"

"I'd rather not," she said quickly.

"What's wrong?"

How could she explain? "I'm not ready to go back to the apartment. Not just yet."

"You're going to have to face the place sooner or later, Syd."

"I vote for later," she told him firmly. She wanted to tell him that it wasn't her apartment. That it had never been her apartment. All she'd brought to her marriage were her clothes and her plants—and her dreams. The only thing left was the plants.

Noah studied her with eyes that saw far more than she wanted to reveal. "I have clothes at my...at the apartment I used to share with Laura and Hannah. It's closer."

"All right."

She closed her eyes against the questions she could almost hear. Without warning, memories sprang from ambush, catching her unaware. She tried to push them aside and couldn't.

If the nurse hadn't come in response to her call...if she hadn't started screaming right away...

Sydney shuddered. She felt Noah touch her arm, but her mind had suddenly shifted, drawing her back inside the bank where bright red blood had stained the white tile floor.

So much blood.

The shots echoed over and over again. She could feel the weight of Jerome's body pressing against hers as they fell, felt her head snap back....

"Sydney! Hey, easy. Take it easy."

"Sorry." She couldn't see his face. Her eyes filled with pools of tears despite her best efforts to hold them at bay. "There was so much blood."

Noah swore softly. "How did we get from clothes to blood? Never mind. It's okay. It's just reaction. Everything's all over."

She tried to tell him that she knew it was okay. That she didn't want to cry. But her throat was clogged with unshed tears, pushing for release.

"I should have done something."

Noah shook his head. "There was nothing you could have done."

He didn't understand. He didn't know how it had been. Jerome telling her how to dress, how to act. Her words bouncing off his anger without impact. Attempts to communicate that failed repeatedly.

She shook her head from side to side. The kaleidoscope of images was becoming all twisted and confused. Noah's hand rested kindly on her shoulder, but she couldn't meet his eyes. Couldn't bear to see his pity.

Jerome was dead, but she was pregnant and someone wanted to hurt her. What was she going to do?

She didn't remember moving, but she found herself sitting on the bed, her face pressed against Noah's hard chest while tears matted his clean white shirt. Fear and horror mingled with hopeless regret. They spilled into racking sobs she couldn't contain.

She cried forever, unable to stop. Only when a teardrop brushed her forehead did she manage to rein in the tide of emotions. Noah was crying too? The idea that this strong man could shed a tear for his brother finally stemmed her own grief.

How Jerome would have loved this scene.

Sydney brushed at her wet face, unable to look at Noah. He stroked her hair then stood and strode into the bathroom. She'd embarrassed him as well as herself.

Water ran in the basin. When he returned, he handed her a damp washcloth. Gratefully, she wiped her face, aware that her damp hair was plastered around it.

"Excuse me." She fled into the bathroom without looking at him.

Noah didn't move as she disappeared. He was as shaken by his own grief as he was by hers.

The hair dryer started and he wondered how she was going to dry her hair with only one hand. Then he decided he didn't care as long as she didn't ask him for help.

He'd thought he had complete control of his emotions—until Sydney came apart in his arms. Her helpless anguish had finally released the grief he had buried right along with his parents, and now his only brother. It was as if Sydney had given him a conduit to his own emotions.

Noah had deliberately fostered the distance between himself and his brother when he was younger. He'd been unable and unwilling to accept Jerome, because it meant accepting his father's infidelity. Noah would live with that regret for the rest of his life.

He couldn't go back, but he could move forward. And forward meant Sydney and the child she carried. She didn't seem to realize that the baby was an unbreakable connection between them. A biological link that meant he would never be able to walk away from his brother's wife.

Part of him was selfishly glad.

Noah expelled a sigh and repacked his bag. He checked the room for loose articles and called the front desk to check out. All he needed was his shaving gear and he'd be ready to go.

The telephone rang.

Noah eyed the instrument with suspicion. "Hello?"

"Major Inglewood? Agent Wickowski. I'm sorry to bother you, but we need to come up and talk with Sydney right away."

"This isn't a go—"

"They fished a man out of the Potomac River a little while ago."

"So?"

"Long hair? Beard? Mustache? Ring a few bells, Major?"

Noah sucked in his breath.

"He was wearing hospital scrubs and carrying Sydney's wallet. Someone shot him in the head at point-blank range."

Chapter Three

Noah gripped the receiver. "Sydney's in the bathroom drying her hair. Why don't we come downstairs? Give us about five—better make it ten minutes."

"Let's make it five, Major."

Noah disconnected and found Sydney watching him warily from the doorway.

"I gather Agent Wickowski wants to ask more questions."

"It's a little more complicated than that."

Her chin lifted. "How much more complicated?"

Noah explained.

Her mouth opened, then closed silently.

"Are you okay?"

"Wonderful." She walked back into the bathroom and the hair dryer started up again. He shouldn't have told her so bluntly. She'd had one shock after another for the past several days. But then, so had he, and she seemed to be handling things just fine.

She came out a few minutes later reinserting her arm into its sling. Her soft brown hair was still damp, but swinging neatly around her shoulders.

Noah stepped past her and added his shaving gear to his duffel bag.

"Better bring the plant," he told her.

"We're leaving?"

"Changing hotels. With the FBI and the police downstairs, I don't think we're going to be anonymous anymore." He didn't add that he'd planned to make the switch even before they arrived. He was operating on instinct here. And his instincts were on full alert. Someone was coming after Sydney.

SITTING INSIDE an empty conference room the hotel had lent them, Agent Wickowski showed them a picture of a man whom Sydney immediately identified as the orderly.

"Could he have been one of the men inside that bank, Mrs. Inglewood?"

"I don't know. Maybe. I just don't know. I'm sorry."

"He had this in his pocket." Wickowski smoothed out a crumpled, torn copy of her wedding picture. Jerome's half had been ripped away, leaving only the smiling bride.

Noah made a noise that sounded like a growl.

"Your fake orderly has a long police record, but unless he recently moved into the big time, bank robbery and murder are out of his league. He's always stuck with petty larceny until now."

"Then he was only in my room to steal?" Sydney asked.

"We're operating on the assumption he was hired to identify your location," Wickowski said. "Several of the local hospitals, including yours, have had a rash of small thefts in the past few days. We recovered most of the stolen items from his apartment, but this picture makes us think you were a specific target. Unless you were carrying this in your purse and he took it for some reason?"

Sydney shook her head, trying to control the fear welling inside her.

"That's what we thought. Since the medical examiner puts his time of death around one this morning, he wasn't your attacker. But he could have been killed right after he met with your attacker, who then went to the hospital."

"Pleasant thought," she said, trying to sound cool and in control. She felt pathetically grateful when Noah touched her arm in silent support.

"You said he was shot?" she asked.

Wickowski inclined his head apologetically. "At close range. Ballistics will tell us if it was one of the guns used in the bank robbery, but I'd say the odds are pretty good. We'd like to take you to a safe house, Mrs. Inglewood."

Sydney had seen a television program about people who had been in police protection and she quickly shook her head. "No. I don't want to be locked up somewhere surrounded by strangers." They would keep her a virtual prisoner.

"We'll assign a female operative—"

"Police protection didn't do me any good at the hospital."

"This time we'll use FBI personnel."

"No." Sydney shook her head, thinking hard. "You said you think my attacker paid this man to find out where I was and then shot him. But my attacker didn't have a gun."

Wickowski frowned at her abrupt change in direction. "How do you know that?"

"Because he didn't shoot me. If he wanted me dead, why didn't he shoot me?"

Noah gazed at her approvingly. The reassurance of his presence helped calm the tension building inside her.

"Mrs. Inglewood—"

"Wickowski," Noah interrupted, "she said no. I'll take

the responsibility for her protection. I plan to stick with Sydney like a second skin."

Sydney bristled. "I don't need to be anyone's responsibility, Noah. I can take care of myself."

Wickowski tried arguments and persuasion, but in the end, the disgruntled agent left them sitting there alone.

"Maybe you should have taken his protection," Noah said.

"No thanks. I'd rather 'hold myself available' for questions." She gave him a weak, lopsided smile. "I thought they only talked like that in B movies."

Noah smiled with his lips, but his expression remained worried. "Let's grab a cab and get you some clothing."

"What about my car? If they haven't towed it, my car is still in the lot behind the jewelry store next to the bank. We can pick it up and save ourselves some cab fare."

Noah hesitated. "I guess it would be all right. I can't imagine the thieves hanging around watching your car, if they even knew which one it was. But are you okay with this?"

"Why wouldn't I be?" Then she realized he meant seeing the bank again since the buildings were side by side. "I promise, I won't freak just seeing the place."

The smile reached his eyes this time. "I can't imagine you freaking over anything."

"Really? I'll let you in on a little secret then. If you want to maintain that belief, keep any and all cockroaches out of my sight."

"I assume we are talking the insect type?"

"Yes. But I'm not crazy about the human variety either."

"I'll keep it in mind."

Her little blue car sat where she'd left it, looking completely normal in a world gone mad. Jerome's fancy sports car, however, was missing from its usual spot, she noticed.

"The police towed Jerome's car," Noah told her without being asked. "I have to collect it from the impound lot. But not today."

She heard him, but couldn't tear her eyes away from the sight of the busy bank. "I can't believe they're open for business as usual—as if nothing happened inside."

When Noah lightly touched her back to guide her to the car, Sydney clamped down on visions of hooded men, guns and blood.

"You okay?"

Determinedly, she closed off the picture of balloons rushing toward the ceiling. "Fine." She settled in the passenger's seat, grateful that Noah was willing to drive. The battle with Wickowski had left her drained and tired again.

Laura's spacious two-bedroom unit was on the top floor of the six-story building. Sydney halted as soon as they turned the corner on her floor.

"What's wrong?" Noah demanded.

He didn't wait for an answer because they could both clearly see the apartment door standing ajar. Someone moved around inside. Noah stepped in front of her as if to shield her from attack.

"Go back downstairs," he whispered.

"No." She gripped his arm as the door swung wide.

Noah shoved her against the wall and spun toward the danger. Only it was Laura who stepped into the hall, her expression going from merely startled to shocked.

"Noah! And Sydney? Oh, my gosh! What are you two doing here?"

Noah strode forward. "I thought you were away."

"I was. I got back this morning." Laura waved off her

explanation. "Never mind that, the apartment was burglarized! The place is a mess."

Noah peered inside, sweeping the overturned furniture with a glance. "Did you call the police?"

"Of course! They've come and gone already. Sydney, are you okay? I've been so worried and... Good grief, what are you wearing? What happened to you?"

"She was attacked in her hospital room early this morning," Noah explained.

"What? Who attacked her? Sydney, are you okay?"

"Let her get inside and sit down," Noah said.

"I can speak for myself," Sydney interjected. "I'm fine, Laura. What happened here?"

Laura shrugged. "The police said they've had a number of apartment break-ins the past few weeks." She led them inside, stepping over a spill of books and CDs near the doorway. "Be careful. You don't want to fall. Should you even be out of the hospital?"

"I'm fine," Sydney reiterated, but it was a lie. Seeing the destructive mess spread before her was twisting her insides into knots of apprehension.

"Be careful there," Laura instructed. "The police said the burglars leave a mess as part of their signature. No finesse, just dump and grab. They're in and out for the cash or valuables."

Noah turned a chair upright for Sydney to sit on. She accepted it gratefully, all her energy draining away. Noah's grim expression spoke louder than words. The responding officers might have considered this a routine break-in, but he didn't.

Neither did she.

"What did they take?" Noah asked.

Laura shook her head. "Nothing, as far as I can determine. Frankly, I'm surprised they didn't leave a donation.

We don't exactly have a lot of stuff in here a thief would want. No cash, and I had my good camera with me, thank heavens."

She waved at the mess. Even pictures had been pulled from the walls.

"They missed my grandmother's diamond brooch and earrings. Now those would have made it worth their time, but I had the jewelry rolled up in a pair of socks. They dumped the drawers without going through the socks."

She shared an ironic smile with Sydney, who explained for Noah's benefit. "She has tons of socks."

"Hey, my feet get cold, what can I say? When I'm not in uniform I like to be comfortable."

"So nothing was taken?" Noah persisted.

Laura shook her head. "Hannah and Bruce already moved most of her stuff to their new place. And my new roommate isn't moving in until next week. It was mostly my things and Sydney's."

"What about photographs?"

Sydney stopped breathing.

Laura stared at Noah as if he'd taken leave of his senses. "Why would a thief want photographs?"

Sydney knew what Noah was asking even before he said the words.

"Do you have a wedding picture of Sydney and Jerome?"

Her lungs refused to expel the air inside them.

"Of course."

"May I see it?"

She exhaled while gripping the armrest with her good hand. Laura crossed the room and began to rummage around.

"Here it is. Why do you want this?"

The glass was cracked and the frame was bent, but the

picture inside was identical to the one the police had taken from the fake orderly. But in Laura's copy, Jerome's half was still intact.

"What's going on, Sydney?" Laura demanded.

Sydney didn't answer. She stared at Noah. Her hand swept the room. "It could be a coincidence."

"I don't like coincidences."

Laura's eyes widened. "You think our burglary has something to do with Sydney's attack? What exactly *did* happen this morning?"

Noah filled her in briskly and Laura went from shock to anger. She hunkered down next to Sydney, taking her friend's good hand and giving it a quick squeeze.

"Oh, Sydney, how awful. But if it's the bank robbers, why are they coming after you? I thought you couldn't identify them."

"I can't."

"She's the only witness left alive," Noah reminded them.

Laura stood up. "I don't get it. Those creeps made off with almost a million dollars. Why aren't they in Brazil or something?"

Noah crossed to the sliding glass door. The balcony looked out over the busy city street below. "We don't know that Sydney was attacked by one of the bank robbers, Laura."

"Well, who else? I thought you didn't believe it was a coincidence."

"I don't." He turned back to Sydney. "Are you sure you don't have an enemy? One you haven't told the investigators about?"

Sydney shook her head. Laura looked exasperated. "An enemy? Sydney? Not a chance. Everyone loves her."

The women exchanged a look that stirred his curiosity to life. They were hiding something.

"Her employers are distraught over what happened," Laura concluded.

Noah watched Sydney. "No irritated customers, ex-lovers, something like that?"

Sydney simply shook her head again.

"That leaves the bank robbers." Noah turned back to the street, studying the pedestrians and parked cars.

"Maybe they don't know she can't identify them," Laura suggested. "Or maybe they just don't want to leave any loose ends."

"Thanks a lot," Sydney said with a weak attempt at humor.

"Sorry. But why else would they come after you?"

"An even better question," Noah said, "is how the men who robbed the bank would know about Sydney's connection to this apartment."

After a second of shock, the two women shared another of those hidden exchanges that said they were holding something back.

"This is no time for secrets, Sydney. You want to tell me what that look is all about?" Noah demanded.

Laura answered quickly. "Sydney was staying here before Hannah's wedding."

Pieces of the puzzle clicked into place. "Why?"

"We were making up wedding favors and doing…well, girl stuff."

"Isn't your apartment only about ten minutes from here?"

Sydney wouldn't meet his eyes.

"You obviously have no idea what goes into planning a wedding," Laura said defensively.

"Who knew Sydney was staying here?"

"Everyone. All our friends, anyhow. It wasn't a secret."

Sydney nodded, but she still wouldn't meet his eyes.

"Noah, are you implying the bank robbers are someone we know?" Laura demanded.

He weighed his words carefully before he answered. "Not necessarily."

"Not necessarily?" Laura squeaked.

"Sydney's identity wasn't revealed by the news media, but it wouldn't have taken much to discover who the surviving victim was."

Laura gaped at him.

"As for learning the location of this apartment, all they had to do was follow you here from the hospital."

Laura jumped, looking spooked. "Follow *me?*"

"Or Hannah. What time did you discover the break-in?"

Laura hugged herself, nervously rocking back and forth on her heels beside the chair he'd righted for her. "I got here around ten, maybe ten-fifteen."

"Then it's possible."

"What is?"

"That the same person who attacked Sydney this morning did this."

"Noah, you're scaring me."

"A little fear might be a healthy thing right now. Sydney managed to summon the nurse so her attacker had to leave in a hurry. It's possible he came here next."

Laura looked at Sydney and back at him, her expression frightened. "Why?"

"Good question."

Sydney met his gaze. "Maybe I was just in the wrong hospital room at the wrong time and the two incidents aren't connected at all."

"He had your picture in his pocket," Noah reminded her.

"Well, what does he want from me?"

"That's the big question," Noah agreed. "Right now, I think we'd better get your things and get out of here. We can discuss possibilities later. Laura, if you'll show me where her stuff is?"

"I can do it myself," Sydney argued. "I'm not helpless."

"Don't strain your voice," Noah admonished. "Although you do sound better."

"She does?" Laura asked.

"Tea's a miracle drug," Sydney whispered.

"Huh?"

Noah relaxed. If she could make a joke, Sydney was handling this latest development pretty well. She struggled to her feet. Noah resisted the impulse that nearly sent him to her side.

"We'll leave as soon as you're ready," he said instead. "I don't think you should stick around here either, Laura. At least not until the police catch whoever did this."

"I hadn't planned to stay after I saw the apartment. I was just waiting for the super to come up with a new door. He said they have to replace this one."

"You're welcome to come with us. I switched hotels and booked a set of adjoining rooms after Sydney fell asleep."

"Thanks, but I called the stewardess making tomorrow's run with me right after I talked to the police. Connie has a place close to the airport. I'm going to spend the night with her. To tell you the truth, now I'm having second thoughts about staying here at all. Ever." She gave a deliberate shiver. "Come on, Sydney. While that's a cute outfit, it isn't really your style. His, I take it?"

Sydney managed a nod while Noah explained she was wearing his favorite jogging outfit.

"I have a feeling it looks much better on you," Laura told him.

Noah cast an appraising eye at Sydney. "I wouldn't necessarily say that."

Laura smiled. "That's what I like, a gentleman. Come on, Sydney, I'll give you a hand getting changed. You have no idea how glad I am to see you up and around. You had us really worried. They wouldn't even let us visit you. Hannah was so upset she didn't want to go to the Virgin Islands with Bruce."

Noah listened to Laura's voice as they headed for the master bedroom. The tone, if not the words, conveyed Laura's nervousness. He prowled the apartment, restlessly setting furniture back on its feet while he waited on the women.

The answering machine blinked silently when he lifted it from the floor. Noah hesitated a moment, then he depressed the play button.

"Laura, it's Gunnar. Give me a call. It's important."

Noah frowned over the unusual name. He'd met a lot of people over the past few days, but no one called Gunnar. Which meant absolutely nothing. Laura was young, single and attractive. There was no reason for him to have met all her friends. He shouldn't have given in to impulse and listened to the tape, but if he was right and Sydney's attack was connected to the bank robbery, what would the robbers want from Sydney?

Unless…

He clenched his teeth, feeling disloyal for what he was thinking. The police and the FBI would check on Jerome and all his acquaintances. They'd also check Sydney and her friends. He couldn't help wondering if one or both of them had known the robbers. The thought was unsettling. He had to hope the FBI knew their job, even if they had fallen short when it came to protecting her.

Protecting her had become *his* mission. Anyone who sought to harm his sister-in-law was going to have to go through him first. He stared at the street below, wishing Sydney would be open with him. He'd already concluded that there was trouble between Jerome and her even before he'd learned she'd been staying with her friends.

Still, she hadn't faked her grief earlier. Whatever their relationship, Sydney had felt something for Jerome.

He bent to right the bookcase and collect the fallen CDs and books. Part of him wished he could just return to duty and throw himself back into work instead of trying to unravel the bits and pieces of this situation, but Sydney and the baby were his responsibility—whether she liked it or not.

"IT'S HARD TO BELIEVE Noah and Jerome are brothers," Laura said, detaching Sydney's hand from the sling so she could get into the cotton sundress they'd selected because its built-in bra made the process easier. There were a lot of things she wouldn't be able to handle one-handed, Sydney realized. Getting dressed was the least of them.

"Noah isn't as good-looking as Jerome, of course," Laura was saying, "yet Noah's got…something. Know what I mean? Is he as nice as he seems?"

Sydney knew what Laura was asking. Over the past few months she'd laid her fears and troubles on her friends' confidential ears.

"Noah has his share of arrogance," Sydney said carefully, "but he can be reasoned with. At least so far."

He was also strangely comforting to have around,

though she didn't add that part. The feelings he aroused in her were much too unsettling.

Laura seemed to understand that Sydney didn't want to discuss Noah. She immediately changed the subject. "You really are a mess, my friend. Look at those bruises."

"Thanks."

"How's your head?"

Sydney pinched the bridge of her nose and offered another lopsided smile. "It hurts." But at least her throat was feeling better.

"Are you really okay? I mean—"

"I know what you mean. I'm fine, Laura. My mind feels a little detached, but that's probably a good thing. It's hard to explain, but I almost feel as if all these events have been happening to someone else. There just hasn't been time to think."

"I'm not surprised. I gather Noah doesn't know? About you and Jerome, I mean?"

Sydney shook her head. "You and Hannah are the only ones who know I was filing for divorce."

"That's what I thought. I won't say anything. It's your business, after all."

Laura had begun collecting Sydney's belongings and folding them into the small green suitcase.

"I'll just take a few days' worth of clothes, Laura. I can come back for the rest later."

"Okay." She paused when she came to the silky turquoise dress and matching shoes. "Why don't I put this in my extra garment bag?"

Sydney had tried to avoid looking at the soft mound of material the intruders had left crumpled on the floor, but the dress pulled her gaze like a beacon. She couldn't hide from her memories any more than she could change the past events. The bridesmaid's dress symbolized the final battle between her and Jerome. A battle she'd known was coming even before he'd seen her trying it on that night.

His autocratic demands had been growing steadily. As had his possessiveness. For someone who had no intention of doing more than giving her an occasional peck on the cheek, he'd become downright controlling in so many ways she'd begun to feel suffocated. The cheerful, out-going man who'd courted her with such determination had begun to disappear completely whenever they were in private. Instead of building a relationship based on their friendship and desire for a family, they'd drawn further and further apart. Talking had done no good. Jerome had become edgy and quick to anger of late. Discussions quickly turned to squabbles that made her heartsick.

The dress had been the final straw. He'd entered her bedroom without knocking and immediately told her to take it off. His wife wasn't wearing something like that in public. The vee cut was far too revealing and the color was all wrong. She'd just have to tell Hannah she couldn't be in the wedding.

Sydney had stared in shock, but Jerome had been completely serious. Curbing her anger, she'd tried to reason with him. Jerome was more irrational than ever. Noah's unexpected call had given her the time she needed to collect some belongings and leave.

She shook her head to rid it of the awful memories and found Laura gazing at her with an expression of pity. "Is there anything I can do for you?"

"You've already done plenty, Laura. Thank you."

"What about the other apartment? I could go over and water your plants and take in the mail."

"You wouldn't mind?"

"No. I've still got the spare key you gave me."

"That would be great. I know I have to go over there and sort through everything, but I'm really not up to that hassle right now."

"No problem." Laura hesitated. "Is it true? About the baby, I mean. Are you really…"

"Pregnant?" Her hand automatically went to her flat stomach. "That's what they told me at the hospital. Only, the clinic doctor—"

"Was a quack. You said so yourself."

"I know."

"That friend of Jerome's didn't know what he was doing. You said the clinic was disorganized and unprofessional."

"I know. It's just that I don't feel pregnant so it doesn't seem real." Events had been swirling around her so fast, her chaotic thoughts hadn't been able to fasten on anything, much less impending motherhood.

"Are you going to keep the baby?"

Sydney opened her mouth in surprise.

"Sorry." Laura bent quickly and zipped Sydney's bag. "It's none of my business. I just wanted you to know you'd be welcome to move back here permanently. I mean, after they catch the robbers and everything. But if you're going to keep the baby, well…" she shrugged. They both knew this was an adults-only complex.

"I don't…I haven't had time to come to terms with being pregnant, let alone given any thought to the future." A future in which she would no longer be alone. But this wasn't the way she had dreamed and planned.

"Hey, I really have lousy timing, don't I?" Laura said in agitation. "You just got out of the hospital, and you're right, you haven't had time to think yet."

No. There hadn't been time to think about any of what had happened.

"Anyhow, I just wanted you to know you have a friend and a place to stay anytime you want it. Hey, how about some earrings?" She held up Sydney's favorite pair of crystal earrings. "And let's try a little lipstick and some blush, okay? Your face is pale as death." Consternation darkened her already pink cheeks. "Oh, blast. I didn't mean to say that."

"It's okay, Laura."

"No, it isn't. I'm normally so controlled. Give me an airplane emergency and I'm unfazed. Let some punk tear my place to shreds and I feel like screaming."

Sydney stood. Suddenly, she wanted out of this room and away from her friend. She needed a quiet spot where she could sort through the chaos in her head.

"Do you want to borrow my green print dress? It's supposed to be hot as Hades tomorrow and that dress also has a built-in bra."

"Okay. Thanks. That would be great." Anything to hurry things along.

Laura gave her arm a gentle squeeze. "I'll get it and be right back."

As Laura opened the door, Noah swung around, a pile of books in his hands. His gaze settled on Sydney. Masculine appreciation crossed his features before his usual mask dropped in place. He set the books down and came toward her in a few short strides.

"Need some help?"

"You can carry my suitcase."

"Is this everything?"

"No," Laura said, coming from her room with a garment bag and a small white shoulder purse. "She'll need this too. I threw in my white silk scarf, Sydney. It'll look good with the dress and cover those bruises on your neck."

"Thank you." She tried to convey all the emotions she was feeling in those simple words and Laura smiled in understanding.

"No problem. Noah, you didn't have to clean up. I'll take care of the mess after I get back from my run on Wednesday."

"Good idea," Noah agreed. "I'm afraid I listened to a message on your answering machine. Someone by the name of Gunnar wants you to call."

"Oh."

"I thought you weren't going to go out with him," Sydney said.

"I'm not. He hasn't called me in a long time. He must have heard about Jerome."

Noah waited.

"He's a friend of Jerome's," Laura explained. "A group of us ran into him at a club one night. He asked me out a couple of times, but he's not really my type."

Sydney nodded agreement. "He's too old for you."

"Yeah. He must be close to forty."

"That old, huh?"

Droll humor played about Noah's lips. Sydney realized Noah was on the long side of thirty-five himself.

"Oops," Laura said with a laugh. "No offense."

"I'm relieved to hear it," he said. "If you ladies are ready to go we'll go down and tell the superintendent we're leaving now."

SYDNEY ENVIED Noah's calm, sure demeanor as he maneuvered her small car through the busy Washington traffic a short time later. Her thoughts swirled helplessly—until she noticed him checking the rearview mirror for a fourth time.

"Is something wrong?"

"Heavy traffic," he replied. "You doing okay?"

"Yes." She hoped people would stop asking her that pretty soon. She wasn't helpless and she wasn't an invalid. She was just—scared.

The familiar landmarks flashed by. How could the rest of the world proceed so calmly as if it were just another day when her entire life had changed so dramatically? Her hand lingered on her stomach. She caught Noah glancing at her and quickly moved her hand away.

"You'll make a good mother," he said.

"Thank you. Motherhood suddenly seems a bit daunting." She smothered a yawn. "And pregnancy makes me unusually tired, I think."

"Your body has been through a lot the past few days, Sydney. Physically, as well as mentally. Don't fight it, you need to rest. I'll have you at the hotel in just a few minutes."

Noah was as good as his word. After handing the valet his keys, he registered them and led her to another bank of elevators. "Come on, sleepyhead. You need to lie down."

Sydney didn't argue. Fatigue canceled out the fear and worry that had plagued her. She let Noah sign them in and guide her to the elevator. As much as she hated to admit it, she was grateful for his support. Even standing seemed like an effort.

He led her into a room and unlocked the connecting door. Vaguely, she remembered him telling Laura he'd gotten two rooms. Too bad Laura hadn't been able to join them. Her friend would have made a good buffer for the attraction she felt for Noah. Plus, she wouldn't have to spend the night alone. She couldn't exactly ask Noah to share a room with her. He was only here with her now because of Jerome. He'd be gone again soon enough.

Stifling a yawn, Sydney followed Noah into the second room and caught herself swaying with fatigue while he turned down the bed.

"Do you need help getting that dress off?"

She thought about what she wasn't wearing underneath and shook her head. "That's okay. I can manage."

"Really?" His eyebrows raised in disbelief.

"Really," she lied. The truth was, she wasn't sure she could even manage the distance between the doorway and the bed, but she wasn't about to tell him that.

"Okay. Holler if you need anything. I'll leave the connecting door ajar."

"Thank you."

Noah tugged back the covers on the bed for her and disappeared inside the other room. She told herself she was grateful that he kept everything so impersonal. It made the situation so much easier, but the truth was, she would have liked to have folded herself into his arms.

And that was a really stupid thought. She was more tired than she'd realized. Sinking down on the bed, she yawned. Forget removing the dress. She'd just lie down for a second.

Her eyes slid shut as exhaustion tugged her down into a deep black well. For one blurry instant, she thought Noah returned, pulling the covers over her. Comforted, she nestled deeper into the pillow. She knew she was dreaming, because he bent and placed a kiss against her hair.

NOAH WATCHED her sleep for several discomfiting seconds. What was she going to do when he told her the truth—or at least what he suspected was the truth? Jerome had lied to her. It was the only explanation.

He rubbed his jaw wearily. Noah didn't want to be

attracted to Sydney Edwards, but he was. And that attraction was going to make a bad situation more awkward when he told her what Jerome had done.

If only she'd been the spoiled wimp he'd expected. Instead, he found himself standing guard over what he suspected was an injured tigress. He hoped that assessment was on target because he didn't think she was anywhere near out of the woods just yet. He was pretty sure a silver Honda had tried to follow them from Laura's apartment. He'd spotted it immediately, but only because he'd been watching for a tail.

He'd seen the car, or one just like it, sitting across the street from the apartment when they'd pulled up. When he'd seen it behind them after they left, he'd driven in circles before heading to the hotel. Fortunately, Sydney had been too tired to notice.

Leaving the door ajar, he went back to his own room and tried not to think about how compelling Sydney looked in sleep. He picked up the telephone and called Agent Wickowski.

Wickowski was not a happy man. He wanted to talk with both of them again.

"Sydney is sound asleep. I'm not going to wake her up just so she can whisper answers to you that you already have. Give us both a break, okay? Let her get some rest."

He listened for a moment, staring down at the busy street below. There was no sign of the silver Honda.

"Look, I called to give *you* some information. Unless you've got a tail on us… Yeah, I didn't think so. I don't have a plate number, but I'm pretty sure someone tried to follow us when we left her old apartment building. Uh-huh. A silver Honda, this year's model. You do know about the break-in at Laura Gooding's apartment, right?"

Wickowski didn't. Noah gave him that information to

brood over and finally hung up. Restless, he tried to settle down with a book he'd been meaning to read, but he couldn't concentrate. In desperation, he turned on the television, seeking a news station. Reading between the lines on an international story, he was surprised his leave hadn't been canceled. And relieved. He would have hated for that to happen right now.

Eventually, he had dinner sent up to the room and went to check on Sydney. She didn't so much as stir. As far as he could see, she hadn't moved since he'd left her. Her hair spilled across the pillow like every man's fantasy. Too bad he wasn't immune to it. The soft rise and fall of her chest told him she was deep in sleep.

When he started thinking about what a nice chest it was, he returned to his room.

Sydney didn't stir when dinner was delivered and Noah didn't have the heart to wake her. He went back to his room and let a game show keep him company over his meal.

Sydney only roused once, groggily, to use the bathroom. Since she didn't call for him, he watched silently from the doorway as she stumbled from the bathroom and fell back into bed. He doubted she even knew he was standing there. She obviously needed sleep more than food, so he left her alone. But he took the image of her in that rumpled sundress into his dreams when he called it an early night.

Hours later, he surged from the bed, abruptly wide-awake. Adrenaline rushed through his system at her broken scream.

Chapter Four

The darkness of the room was complete. Sydney lay still, wondering what had awakened her to such heart-pounding fear. A raging thirst burned in her throat. Abruptly, she remembered where she was and why. That accounted for the adrenaline rush pumping through her body.

Until she realized she wasn't alone in the room.

Someone moved stealthily towards the bed. Her gaze flashed to the connecting door. Instinctively, she knew the person in the room with her wasn't Noah.

Sydney rolled from the bed, but the assailant was faster. Before she could draw in a breath to scream, he'd rushed her, bridging the distance between them in a heartbeat. She tried to twist away, out of his grasp, but he was lean and snake quick.

The recognizable smell of garlic assailed her. He wrestled her back down onto the bed. New terror gripped her when his hand landed on her breast. She tried to squirm free but his weight came down on top of her, forcing the air from her lungs.

Terrified, she bit his arm hard enough to draw blood.

"Bitch!"

He slapped her, jarring her head with the force of the blow. In desperation, Sydney jerked her head forward. She was rewarded by a grunt when her forehead struck his face. She clawed at the ski mask covering it, even as she found the air to scream.

The cry came out a broken croak of sound, but it was enough. The man hesitated. Sydney didn't. She swung her cast, trying for his face again, now partially exposed by the dislodged ski mask. He rolled off her and away with astounding speed. The blow glanced off his forearm instead of smashing his face as she'd hoped. The mask came off as he ran for the door.

The intruder fled out the hall door, giving Sydney a glimpse of dark hair and an unshaved jawline as he fled into the light. She drew in another breath to scream for Noah when the connecting door swung wide with a jarring crash. Her breath expelled in an involuntary cry as Noah charged into her room.

"Sydney!"

"He went down the hall!" The words came out on a choked sob. She was shaking all over.

"Wait here."

"No, wait!" But as Sydney struggled from the bed, Noah ran into the hall. Fear for his safety sent her feverishly hunting in the dark room for the telephone—until it occurred to her to turn on the light. In the soft glow of the lamp, she calmed.

Her face and head throbbed. So did her hand beneath the cast, but otherwise she was unhurt. She tried for calm, while she concentrated on trying to decipher the printed instructions for the phone. She pressed the symbol for the front desk.

"Good morning, this is Leighton. May I help you?"

Desperately, she tried to swallow past her dry throat. "Yes." The word came out sounding like sandpaper. "Someone just broke into my room."

"Broke into your room?" the voice asked incredulously.

"Noah is chasing him, but what if he has a gun?"

New fear blotted out the clerk's startled response as someone pounded on her door.

"Sydney!"

"Noah!" She dropped the receiver and ran to let him inside. Only after she opened the door did she realize Noah had been running through the hotel stark naked.

"We need to call security."

"I've got the front desk on the phone."

"Good."

A very naked, very angry Noah stalked across the room, totally unconcerned by his nudity.

She tried hard not to stare, but he resembled some sort of Greek god come to life. Unbidden, her gaze traced a path over his lightly furred chest and lean hips that tapered to a thatch of hair from which sprang...

Quickly looking away, she glimpsed a flash of droll humor in Noah's otherwise darkly stormy eyes.

"You're naked."

"When I heard you scream, I didn't take time for the niceties." Retrieving the fallen receiver, he spoke with quiet authority. "This is Noah Inglewood. Get security to meet the descending elevator right now," he demanded. "You'd better call the police as well. I'll be right down."

He hung up without waiting for a response. "Are you okay?"

She nodded, trying to focus on his face, but a naked Noah Inglewood was impossible to ignore. "Uh..." Embarrassment paralyzed her vocal cords. It was impossible to ignore his semierect state.

"Wait here." He crossed to the connecting door giving

her a good view of a slim waist, strong legs and nicely rounded buttocks.

He returned seconds later, fastening his pants. A white dress shirt was draped over his shoulder while his bare feet were stuffed into a pair of spit-polished dress shoes.

"Are you sure you're okay?"

She managed to nod.

"He didn't touch you?"

She shook her head. "No. I mean, yes." She hadn't thought eyes could get that dark.

"But I'm fine."

His hand cupped her face. The gesture was amazingly tender. So was his expression. Her heart began its wild tattoo once again.

"Tell me what happened."

His quiet authority released the dam of words.

"Something woke me and I realized someone was in the room. I tried to get away, but he knocked me back onto the bed. We struggled and I bit him. Then I butted him in the face with my head. I think I hit his nose. I hope I broke it. When I hit him with my cast, he took off."

Her voice sounded thin and shrill and she was still shaking all over in delayed reaction. Noah cradled the back of her head and pulled her gently against his chest. The gesture was meant to offer comfort. Instead, it sent shock waves through both of them as her cheek connected with his bare skin. Noah instantly released her.

"Sorry." He pulled on his shirt, never taking his eyes from her. "I hope you broke his nose, too. You're pretty incredible, you know that?" He said it with a tight smile.

"Noah, it was the same man."

Noah stilled.

''I could smell the garlic. He reeks of it, Noah. And I pulled his ski mask off.''

Noah turned back toward the bed.

''Over there. On the floor.''

Noah walked over and looked at it, but he didn't pick it up. ''Did you see his face?''

''No. It was too dark and I was too scared. But he has dark hair and he needs a shave. I saw that much when he ran out into the hall.''

''You did great. Wait in my room, Sydney. Lock the connecting door and don't open either door until you hear me call your name, all right?''

She managed to bob her head in answer.

His thumb caressed her bottom lip. Then he was gone. Sydney stared after him, badly shaken all over again. Her lips tingled where he'd touched them and she couldn't quite seem to catch her breath. His touch was electrifying and she craved it.

She hurried into Noah's room and locked the door, checking the hall door to be sure it was locked as well. Her life had turned into one of those dumb horror movies where everything happened too fast to comprehend.

She sank down on Noah's bed and tried to stop shaking. The sheets were still warm from the imprint of his body. The faint scent of his cologne teased her senses and the vision of him coming to her rescue like some naked warrior refused to step aside for the raft of other thoughts waiting for her attention.

She needed to get control here. She had just been assaulted. She could not be attracted to Noah. She would not *allow* herself to be attracted to Noah.

It was the stress, she decided. Anyone would be stressed by all that had happened. Nothing had been the same in her world since the day Laura had introduced her to Jerome.

Jerome was dead and she needed to start concentrating on staying alive herself. It was time to draw on all that self-reliance she'd learned when it had been just Grandma and her. She composed her features and headed for the bathroom. Water soothed her thirst, and washing her face helped steady her a little, even if there was still a decided tremor in her hands.

At least she was starting to think again, though she didn't like the thoughts she was having. The bank thieves had shown no hesitation when it came to shooting helpless victims. Yet twice now, someone had come after her and she was still alive.

"Why?" She stared at her reflection in the bathroom mirror, seeing no answers in the pale features staring back at her. Lightly she touched the reddened imprint where he'd struck her.

What did he want from her?

"Sydney?" Noah called out as he rapped on the door. She hurried to unlatch it for him.

"You okay?" Noah demanded. His eyes snapped angrily as he took in the red mark on her cheek. She was glad that anger wasn't directed at her.

"Yes."

"The police are on their way. Hotel security wants to talk to you. Are you up to it?"

Sydney nodded. "Did he get away?"

"More than likely." Noah sounded disgusted. "They're combing the building, but the elevator was empty when it reached the ground floor. No one noticed where else it stopped. He may still be somewhere in the building, but one of their people saw a man with dark hair take off on a motorcycle. Security, of course, didn't get a plate number or a description.''

No wonder Noah was angry. She had a feeling he wasn't used to losing at anything.

"Tell me again exactly what happened.''

As she did, his anger deepened and she realized it was self-directed. "I'm sorry, Sydney. I thought I could protect you.''

She laid her hand on his biceps, feeling the tension that practically vibrated from him. "You did. He left, didn't he?''

"Only after you clobbered him. How's your hand?''

She withdrew her touch and tried to smile. "It's throbbing, but I don't think I did any real damage. I just don't understand why this is happening.''

Noah didn't reply. His expression packed a volume of words in that simple look.

"Hey, I don't know what he wants.''

Noah's stillness was unnerving. Where another man might fidget or pace, Noah didn't exhibit any of the usual mannerisms. He regarded her in motionless silence.

Sydney allowed her irritation to grow. "Look, if your attitude is supposed to intimidate me, it's not going to work. I don't have a clue what's going on here.''

"Take it easy.''

"How am I supposed to do that?''

"You're right. I'm sorry, Syd.''

"Sydney.''

"Sydney,'' he agreed. "It would have helped if you'd gotten a better look at the guy.''

"Sorry. Next time I'll ask him to pose for pictures.''

His lips quirked. "I'm the one who's sorry. At least you got his ski mask. That should give the police something to work from. Maybe they can match hairs from the cap to the bastard.''

"They'll have to catch him first. If it was the same man from the hospital, how did he know I was here, Noah?"

"There was a silver Honda outside Laura's apartment. I thought I lost it, but I guess not. The good news is, I gave Wickowski the plate number.''

"Why didn't you tell me?"

"There wasn't anything you could have done except worry.''

"Yeah, with good reason as it turns out. What about Laura?"

"He doesn't want Laura. He wants you.''

"Why?'' Uncomfortably, she began to pace, her thoughts tumbling faster than she could form the words. "Noah, what if…well, what if one of the men in the bank that day was more than just a thief?"

"What do you mean?"

She pivoted. "Let's say they learned I wasn't dead and decided to kill me. But what if the one who came after me wanted to rape me first?''

Noah swore. "He touched you?"

"Just my breast. It might have been accidental. We were struggling. But if it wasn't.…''

His expression was thunderous.

"I only wondered because he was practically on top of me before I scared him off.''

"We need to let Wickowski know about this. It might narrow down the search if they have a known bank robber with a history of rape as well.''

He rubbed his jaw, drawing her attention to the morning stubble on his cheeks, which gave him a decidedly dangerous look.

"I find it hard to believe he went after you in the hospital intending to rape you."

So did she when he put it like that. "Then give me another explanation. Why didn't he simply kill me?"

"I don't know."

"Me either, but I'm getting real tired of this. Let's get out of here, Noah."

"And go where?"

"I haven't got a clue."

Sidney sank down stiffly on his bed, aware of every ache in her body, including an expanding headache. She would *not* let Noah see how upset she was. She had never given in to public displays of any sort and she wasn't going to start now, even if all she wanted to do was bury her head in his pillow and cry.

"Sydney, do you have a friend or some distant family member you could stay with?"

Sydney shook her head.

"All right." His voice gentled. "Security will be here any minute to talk to you."

"I'd like to change clothing first." She was not going to face another inquisition dressed in rumpled clothing.

His brows pleated, but he didn't argue or ask why. "Do you want help?"

"No."

Not even if she needed it. Her emotions were seesawing all over the place, and the last thing she wanted was for Noah to touch her right now.

"Okay. I'll direct the men in here while you go back in your room and change."

"Fine." She kept her mind as blank as possible, not looking toward the bed. Getting out of the sundress proved harder than getting into it, and the green dress was impossible. The zipper defeated her completely. She couldn't close it one-handed no matter how she tried.

Frustration nearly brought tears to her eyes. She blinked them back furiously. All she needed to do was select another outfit from her suitcase, but childishly, she didn't want a different outfit. She wanted to face Noah and the police looking calm and professional, instead of like some out-of-control victim.

She straightened her shoulders and marched to the connecting door. Masculine voices came from the other side. She cracked the door open and called out.

"Noah? Could I see you a minute?" Instantly, he appeared. She stepped back as he slipped inside, closing the door behind him.

"I can't reach the zipper."

She was proud of her matter-of-fact tone. Even prouder that she didn't so much as twitch under his touch. Not even when his knuckles brushed her bare skin, sending ridiculous tremors right through her.

He nodded toward the white silk scarf lying on the end of the bed. "Would you like me to wrap that around your neck for you?"

"That depends. Are you still angry?"

He didn't smile at her attempted humor. "Not at you, Sydney."

She stood still while Noah carefully twisted the silky material lightly around her neck, draping the ends over her shoulder. She tried to keep her eyes glued on the picture hanging over the bed in an unsuccessful effort not to notice how good he smelled or how badly she wanted to throw herself into the security of his arms.

"Thank you."

His gaze bored into hers, causing things to flutter that had no business fluttering. The pull of awareness between them was almost frightening because she clearly saw that it wasn't one-sided. An answering flame burned in his normally controlled features before he extinguished the look with the blink of his eyes.

"You're welcome," he said calmly with no trace of the sensual volcano she had glimpsed churning beneath his surface calm. "All set?"

"Yes." But she resented his control when her own was so shaky. His hand hesitated at her back, triggering more ripples of reaction low in her gut. She would get her crazy emotions under control if it killed her.

Noah had to give her credit. Sydney never once took a coy or flirtatious stance with him. She'd matter-of-factly asked his help getting the dress zipped and stood patiently while he'd fiddled with the scarf, trying to keep his hands as impersonal as possible. She looked cool, calm and serenely unapproachable.

Obviously, the intimacy of the situation didn't bother her a bit. It was Noah's mind that skittered away from thoughts of her incredibly soft skin everywhere he'd touched her. Sydney was having a terribly disturbing effect on him and he didn't like it one bit. Protecting her was one thing. That was duty. But noticing her as an attractive woman was something else altogether. When was he going to get it through his head that she was off-limits?

Sydney's emotions and the situation were getting to him. She hadn't faked her grief yesterday. Or her fear this morning. And she seemed truly puzzled by the most recent events. As was he. None of what was happening made any sense.

Noah didn't like things that didn't make sense.

Men with enough smarts to pull off the bank heist and get away clean should have been much more adroit at killing the only eyewitness. Therefore, they didn't want her dead. So what *did* they want?

He wasn't buying into the security people's explanation—not for a second. Maybe D.C. did have a rapist who had attacked several women inside hotel rooms, but the odds against that individual singling out Sydney right now were astronomical.

What bothered him the most was how the guy had found them. It was possible they'd been followed from Laura's apartment, as he'd told Sydney. But that didn't explain how the man learned which room she was in. The obvious answer was that he had bribed the night clerk. Leighton struck him as the sort who'd turn his head for a few bucks. If so, they'd probably never know. Leighton wouldn't risk his job by admitting as much to the police.

The first police officer who arrived on the scene agreed with him, as did Agent Wickowski. Wickowski decided a trip to his office was called for and Noah was surprised when Sydney didn't even object.

Once inside the building, the two of them were separated. Noah found himself in an interrogation room answering questions. Most of those related to Sydney and his brother. He responded stoically, knowing the men were simply doing their job, but as time stretched, he became increasingly concerned for Sydney.

"Look, I understand your questions and the reasons for them, but my sister-in-law is pregnant. She's been through a lot the past few days. Do you seriously think she's in collusion with the men who pulled that robbery?"

"No, sir, but we have to look at all the possibilities."

"Understood, but the woman just left the hospital. She's had one traumatic event after another. How much longer are you planning to keep us here?"

"It shouldn't be long now, sir. Excuse me for a few minutes."

There wasn't much else he could do. He eyed the bitter coffee and the sweet doughnuts in disgust. He hoped they'd offered Sydney something more palatable. Everyone knew pregnant women should avoid caffeine.

Noah glanced at his watch, amazed to see how much time had elapsed. He'd give the agent five more minutes and then he was going to start issuing his own orders.

"Major? Sorry for the delay." Wickowski stepped into the room, holding the door open in clear invitation. Noah walked forward quickly.

"Mrs. Inglewood is giving a formal statement right now," Wickowski said as they entered the hall. "Would you like to go down to the cafeteria and grab a bite to eat while we wait?"

"What about Sydney?"

"We sent a tray up for Mrs. Inglewood. She's being most cooperative." He slanted Noah an odd glance. "She's a strong individual. I'm not sure I'd be able to view these events with such equanimity."

His words jarred, striking an odd tone. "Agent Wickowski, if you're trying to ask me something, ask it straight out. I may not know Sydney very well, but I've observed her at close hand under some pretty extreme situations the past few days, and I'd stake my commission on the fact that she had nothing to do with that bank robbery."

"I agree with you, Major."

"Then why take that tone?"

Wickowski pressed the button for the elevator. "Your colonel speaks quite highly of you. Your record speaks for itself."

Noah wasn't surprised they'd been checking on him. If

anything, he was relieved to see they were being thorough. The elevator doors parted to reveal a crowd already bent on the cafeteria. The two didn't speak again until they stood in the noisy food line.

"Your training and military standing put you in a perfect position to offer us some insight into these events, Major."

"And Sydney in particular?"

Wickowski smiled. "Exactly. She's taking the death of her husband quite well."

"Yes, she is." Noah waited.

"Did you know she planned to file for divorce?"

If the man had intended to shock him, he was in for a disappointment. Noah had already questioned their relationship in his own mind. "I never met Sydney until after Jerome was killed."

"And your brother didn't suggest they were having problems?"

The line moved forward and Wickowski was diverted, placing his order. Noah had no appetite, but he ordered a sandwich and a soft drink.

"I've already told you everything my brother said to me, pretty much verbatim. However, Sydney told me she was staying with her friends and not at their apartment prior to the robbery."

"But not that she planned to file for divorce," Wickowski prodded.

"No. I suspect she felt that was none of my business as well as totally irrelevant, given the situation. What did you get on that plate number I gave you?"

"The car was stolen."

Noah wasn't surprised.

They paid for their meals and Wickowski led the way

to a newly vacated table. "Your brother lived an expensive life-style, Major."

"We've been over this already. I know very little about my brother's life-style."

Wickowski chomped on a pickle strip and waved it in the air. "Do you believe your brother could have been coerced into helping with this robbery?"

Noah didn't hesitate. "Yes."

Wickowski choked on the pickle. After a hasty swig of his drink, he managed to control the coughing spell that followed.

"As I told you earlier," Noah said calmly, "my brother was spoiled. He liked getting his own way. If he needed money and thought he saw a way to get some illegally without being caught, I think it's possible he would at least consider the option."

The man set down his glass, his expression intent. "Thank you for your honesty. I'm going to tell you something, Major. Something I want you to hold in strict confidence."

When he paused, obviously waiting, Noah agreed.

"There have been a series of these robberies. One in Maryland, one in the district and two in Virginia. In every case, only one bank employee was inside at the time. In every case, that employee died at the scene or shortly thereafter. Each victim tended to live over and above his means."

Noah couldn't summon any surprise over this news. "A lot of people do that."

"True enough. We have no proof any of the victims were involved. In fact, we have no leads of any kind, Major. Until Sydney survived, we didn't even know how many people were involved in these crimes. She's our only link."

"Then I would have thought you'd have taken better care of her from the outset."

The tips of Wickowski's ears reddened, but he didn't rise to the bait.

"So, why haven't they killed her?" Noah asked.

Wickowski leaned back in his chair. "That's what we're hoping you can find out for us."

Noah narrowed his eyes.

"Mrs. Inglewood doesn't want our protection, but she seems to accept yours. We want to use that."

"You mean you want me to help you use her as bait?"

"I mean that if she won't let us protect her, I want to know who comes after her. Because they will, Major. You've already seen that for yourself. They want something from her and we want whatever it is they want."

"And what if she's right that one of the robbers is also a rapist?"

"We're looking into that. We need you to keep her alive." He leaned forward intently. "Find out what the robbers want from her. Then help us get it first."

Noah pushed aside his plate. "You don't want much, do you?"

"Wouldn't you do this anyhow, Major?"

The question still rankled hours later when he and Sydney were driven back to the hotel to collect her car and their luggage. Sydney had been uncharacteristically silent the whole time.

"Are you all right?" Noah asked, darting a glance in her direction as he pulled out into the heavy traffic.

"You know, I'm really sick of that question. No offense, but it seems to be the first thing everyone says to me."

His lips twitched and she twisted to face him more

fully. "Tell me something, Noah. What exactly do you do in the military?"

"Why do you ask?"

"It was hard not to notice how deferentially they started treating you. I realize you're just a bystander here, but even so. Did they ask you to spy on me?"

Noah choked on a bubble of laughter. "Wickowski didn't give you nearly enough credit," he told her. "I'm supposed to keep you alive until we find out what these guys want from you."

From the corner of his eye, he saw her shoulders slump. "And once you know that, it's okay if they kill me?"

He braked for the red light and turned to face her, lifting her chin. "No one is *ever* going to hurt you again. You got that?" he growled.

The car behind him beeped to signal the light had changed. Noah ignored the driver. He pinned her with his stare, willing her to believe him. Finally she nodded. He couldn't tell if she was relieved or simply scared.

"You'd better drive on before we get a ticket for loitering."

Her voice was thick, but there was determination in her expression. Damned if her vulnerability wasn't getting to him. He ran his thumb across her lower cheek in a deliberate caress before dropping his hand and focusing on traffic.

"Where are we going?" she asked him quietly.

"Ever hear of a place called Fools Point?"

"Yes. You and Jerome grew up there." She frowned. "Why are we going there?"

"Because despite its proximity to D.C., it's still small-town America. Everybody knows everybody else and strangers stand out."

"You want us to stand out?"

"No. I told you, I intend to keep you safe. Dad's house is there. It's unlikely anyone will connect you with the place, at least right away. Let's call it my version of a safe house. I'm hoping it will be better than a motel or hotel. Do you have a better idea?"

"No," she said reluctantly.

She sat back, looking totally composed and detached, much the way she'd looked ever since the break-in this morning. Her calm bothered him because he suspected it was artificial. She should have been huddled in some corner, mindless with fear.

"Do you want something to eat first?" he asked.

"Not really. They gave me a sandwich and some doughnuts."

"I guess the FBI are just plain old cops when it comes right down to it."

They shared a weak smile.

Sydney watched Noah calmly thread his way through the dense traffic and decided he had wonderful hands. Long, graceful fingers that rested as lightly on the steering column as they did on a woman's skin.

She brushed aside the direction of that thought and stared at the traffic beside them. They were getting out of town right ahead of rush hour, but Noah's eyes kept flicking to the rearview mirror.

"Trouble?"

Noah shook his head. "I'm just being cautious. I told Wickowski where we were going, but I thought they might have given us a silent escort anyhow."

"How would you know the bad guys from the good guys?"

Noah grinned, reducing the tension lines around his eyes. "The good guys won't shoot at us or try to run us off the road."

"How reassuring."

As if to put her at ease, Noah began asking questions about her job. He appeared genuinely interested in her replies. He wasn't quite as forthcoming about his own work, but she suspected there might be security reasons for that. The FBI had definitely treated him as if he was someone not to mess with. She hoped the bank robbers would view him the same way.

Despite her own situation, Sydney found herself relaxing for the first time in months. "I should call my boss and let him know I don't know how soon before I'll be back to work."

"You can call when we get to town," Noah promised.

She wished Noah's presence weren't so comforting.

Comforting? Who was she trying to fool? Noah was wickedly attractive in a pulse-pounding way that made her all too aware that she was most definitely a woman. She couldn't keep skirting the knowledge of her attraction to him. She simply couldn't act on it. Now if they'd met a year ago, before Jerome was anything more than the man who worked next door at the bank—but they hadn't, and Noah was off-limits. Forbidden fruit.

A man she could easily have loved.

"Did you love Jerome?"

The question jerked her around in her seat. "What sort of question is that?" she snapped guiltily.

"Wickowski said you were planning to file for divorce."

"Wickowski has a big mouth."

"Want to talk about it?"

"No. Do you want to talk about your relationship with your brother?"

She'd caught him so completely off guard, he nearly missed the 270 exit. She felt guilty, but only a little. Despite their rocky relationships with Jerome, she knew Noah grieved for his brother.

"He idolized you, you know."

Noah snorted. "Not likely."

"Oh, but he did. I think he also resented you. He felt you'd given him an impossible standard to live up to."

"He said that?"

"Not in so many words, but Jerome was complicated. I never really understood him at all."

He waited, but she didn't say anything else.

"You didn't answer my question," he said finally.

"No."

She saw his jaw clench. "No, you didn't answer my question, or no, you didn't love him?"

"Why ask the question at all, Noah?"

He expelled a deep breath and kept his eyes on the road. Her nonanswer was answer enough. "Call it curiosity."

"I don't want to discuss this, Noah."

"Do you agree that you're in danger?"

"Yes."

"Do you think the bank robbery and your attacks are connected?"

"I..." She cursed softly. "They must be or else I've got some really bad karma going for me right now."

"I'm going to take care of you, Sydney."

"Why?"

He didn't respond right away. They rode in troubled silence until Noah took the off-ramp for Fools Point. Sydney had only been here once on her way to the fertility clinic with Jerome. She wondered if the sleepy little town had changed much since Noah had grown up here. Jerome claimed it was as it had always been, but she knew it wouldn't be much longer before developers got their hands on all the open land surrounding the town and

changed the landscape the way they'd done with Gaith-
ersburg and Germantown.

Noah stopped for the traffic light in the center of town
and leveled a long look at her face.

"There's no one answer to your question, Sydney. I
care about you. And your baby..."

He hesitated. Sydney realized this was the first time
she'd ever seen Noah uncertain.

"Your baby is the only family I have left. I don't intend
to let anything happen to either one of you."

She was strangely disappointed in that answer. He was
holding back something.

"So protecting me is your duty?"

His jaw set and his eyes bored into her.

"The light's green now, Major."

He started to say something else and stopped. Without
another word, he turned onto Perry Road past the doctor's
office where Jerome had stopped before driving to the
clinic that day.

Not wanting to be reminded of that event, she stared at
the old stone church instead. Jerome told her it had been
there since the eighteen-hundreds. But she couldn't focus
on anything because she was so aware of the man at her
side.

Noah turned left onto a side street and slowed the car.
He came to an abrupt stop in the road, staring toward the
large gray frame house Jerome had pointed out to her that
same day. The house sat back from the road with a long
sweeping lawn that led to a wide covered porch spanning
the front of the house. The hedges needed to be trimmed
and weeded and the house itself could have used a coat
of paint, but it was a lovely old structure all the same.

Noah tensed, circling the cul-de-sac before coming to
a stop opposite the house.

"Noah? What's wrong?"

"Jerome said the tenants were supposed to vacate last week."

She followed the direction of his stare and apprehension sank its tendrils deep inside her. Three vehicles sat in the driveway. Two pickup trucks and one motorcycle.

Hadn't hotel security seen someone speed away on a motorcycle shortly after her attack this morning?

Chapter Five

The front door opened and a leanly muscled man in a T-shirt and jeans stepped onto the porch. The jeans were old, paint-stained and torn. An obviously empty can of paint dangled from one hand as he came down the steps and sauntered over to the white panel truck. Trouble looking for a place to happen.

Noah turned to Sydney. "Wait here while I check this out."

"I'm coming with you."

"No. Let me check it out first." Probably he was overreacting, but security had seen a motorcycle driving away fast from the hotel this morning, so his mind was making connections where maybe none existed.

Her eyes flashed with annoyance, but his tone must have warned her that the subject wasn't up for debate. Or maybe she didn't like the tough looks of the man any more than he did. Either way, she remained seated as he climbed from the car.

The man placed the paint can in the back of the panel truck and whirled around at Noah's approach, braced for trouble.

Noah's heart sped up as he came to a stop several feet away. The man's face showed faint traces of bruising, and if Noah wasn't mistaken, there was tape under his shirt. A broken rib or two? This guy had either been in a recent fight or an accident.

"Help you?" the man asked in a deceptively quiet voice. From beneath a mane of thick black curling hair, badly in need of a cut, his dark eyes took Noah's measure.

"Yeah. You can tell me who you are and what you're doing here. I'm Noah Inglewood."

Acknowledgment flickered in his eyes.

"Jerome's brother?"

"That's right. I was led to believe the house was empty."

"It is. Jerome hired us." He inclined his head in the direction of the logo on the side of the truck. Yosten Lumber.

The self-assured toughness about the man kept Noah on guard. He stood easily, arms relaxed, but he was balanced on the balls of his feet, ready to move quickly if he needed to. There was something disturbingly familiar about the guy.

"Jerome's dead," he told the stranger. "Do I know you?"

The man didn't seem surprised by the news, but he definitely appeared surprised by the question.

"We've met, but it was a long time ago."

Noah waited.

A wry sort of humor settled lightly on the man's lips. He gave a slight inclination of his head as if conceding something. "Alex Coughlin. Your brother and I were classmates."

Noah placed the name after a second. Though Noah hadn't lived here at the time, he knew the Coughlin kid had been well on his way to building a reputation as reckless. Apparently, he'd finished the project.

"I was sorry to hear about Jerome," Coughlin added with a serious expression.

"Hey, Alex," someone yelled from inside the house. "You comin' back in today or…? Oh. Company?"

Noah eyed the newcomer and his unease grew. The greasy-haired man who stepped onto the porch had a long, pointy ferret face and a mouth that turned down at the corners. Like Alex, he was dressed in a decrepit pair of jeans, but instead of a white T-shirt, he wore a sleeveless black one to display an impressive cobra tattoo coiled up one leanly muscled arm. There was a bandage on the other arm.

Noah had seen his type before. Anyone who'd ever watched a cop show had seen his type. A tough guy.

Ferret Face rubbed absently at a recent bruise on his chin and stared hard.

"Barry Fairvale, meet Noah Inglewood," Alex Coughlin said easily. "Jerome's brother."

The squinty eyes narrowed even further without a shred of welcome. "That right? His brother, huh? Military type, right?"

This guy was going to be trouble. "That's right."

The head bobbed as the eyes continued to measure him. "Shame about Jerome getting offed like that," he said. But his calculating expression wasn't saying anything of the kind.

A warning prickle went down Noah's back. He'd have taken bets that Barry Fairvale had seen the inside of more than one jail cell. And that thought reminded him that Sydney waited in the car at his back. Would she be smart enough to take off if things went bad? Because he had a strong hunch they just might any second now. All of his instincts were on full alert.

A voice yelled from inside the house and Noah wondered just how many of them there were. He should have taken Sydney away from here the moment he spotted that motorcycle.

"What the hell are you two doing out there? Is that bathroom finished yet?"

"Company, Gun," Fairvale said without turning around.

The screen door banged open. The man who filled the space was older than the other two. Older and harder. Years of outdoor work had toughened his body and put age lines on his face. His cold gray stare absorbed the scene.

"This here's Jerome's brother," Fairvale announced.

Noah wouldn't have been surprised to see Fairvale spit or start scratching. Either action would have been as much of an act as the dumb hick routine. Feral intelligence shone in Fairvale's eyes.

The blond newcomer started down the steps.

"Jerome's brother? Why didn't you say so?"

He came forward with his hand outstretched and an obliging smile pasted on his face. Noah suspected he was the most dangerous of the three.

"Noah, right?"

Noah waited, instinctively braced for trouble. "That's right."

"I'm Gunnar Yosten. I'm a friend of Jerome's—was a friend, that is. Real sorry to hear about what happened to him. Real sorry. I've been out of town. Didn't hear the sad news until the other day. I've been trying to find some way to get hold of his wife ever since. That her, in the car?"

Gunnar wasn't exactly a common name in the D.C. area, and the voice matched the voice on the answering machine in Laura's apartment. No wonder she hadn't thought this man was her type. Despite his looks and the affable front, he wasn't any smart woman's type. Nothing could hide the cold calculation behind his friendly facade.

Noah bristled at the way Yosten stared toward the car, and he took a step forward to block that view without extending his hand. "Why don't you tell me what the three of you are doing here?"

Gunnar's eyes narrowed. His expression stayed friendly as he dropped his hand to his side. He wore the same uniform as the other two, stained jeans and a T-shirt. This one was too dirty to call white.

"Sure. I imagine it is a bit disconcerting to find us here when you weren't expecting it."

"You could say that," he agreed tightly.

"Jerome hired us to fix the place after the tenants moved out. He said he was planning to move here with his wife. That's why I've been trying to reach her. I didn't want to disturb her right now, but I need to know how far she wants us to take the renovations, what with Jerome's death and all."

Noah was more wary than ever. The explanation would have been entirely plausible if Sydney and Jerome had been happily married, but they hadn't even been living together.

"The house passes to me, not his wife."

"That so?"

Noah nodded, aware that Coughlin had moved away from the truck and was heading toward the motorcycle—or else down the driveway toward Sydney.

"I didn't realize that. I guess it's you I need to talk to then."

"Yes." He resisted an impulse to look over his shoulder and watch Coughlin. He felt confident Sydney wouldn't let the guy anywhere near her, and he was pretty sure it would be Gunnar who would signal the start of any trouble.

"I'll need some time to look over the place before I determine what sort of renovations I want to undertake. I can see you've been busy," Noah conceded, "and I'll reimburse you for whatever work you've already done, but I'm going to have to ask that you stop for now."

The cold eyes grew colder.

"Why don't you give me an itemized invoice for the work you've completed and a list of what Jerome wanted done. I'll call after I have a chance to review the situation."

Gunnar Yosten reined in his unhappy expression. "I'll do that," he promised.

Stepping to one side to bring Coughlin into view over his shoulder, Noah realized Coughlin had stopped beside the motorcycle. Unfortunately, that put him between Noah and Sydney. Fairvale still lounged against the porch rail. His eyes were trained on Sydney's car. These men might be exactly who and what they said they were, but the atmosphere was all wrong.

"Guess that means we're done here for today," Coughlin called out from behind him.

"Yes," Noah agreed decisively before Yosten could respond.

"Okay by me," Coughlin said cheerfully. "The bathroom's painted and you'll remember I told you I needed to leave early today anyhow. Call me later, Gun."

Coughlin slid a leg casually over his bike.

Noah brought his attention back to Gunnar Yosten.

Gunnar looked toward the porch. "Barry, grab the rest of the equipment. Looks like we're leaving early, too. I'll be in to give you a hand in a minute."

Fairvale disappeared inside with a grunt. The air remained charged with a sense of suppressed violence. Noah had no trouble picturing these three robbing a bank—or coming after Sydney. If there were weapons inside the house, Noah knew he was in big trouble.

The motorcycle kicked to life. With a roar of sound, it backed down the driveway.

"I'll just go over and pay my respects to Jerome's wife."

Noah caught Gunnar's arm. "Sydney's not up to talking with anyone right now. I'm sure you understand." He wasn't letting any of these men near her.

Yosten looked down at the hand clamped around his arm and back up at Noah. His anger was controlled, but visibly there. He was bigger than Noah and more muscular, but Noah felt confident he could handle Yosten. It would only get dicey if anyone else entered the mix. Or if they were armed.

For a second, he and Gunnar eyed each other in open animosity. Then, with a measuring stare that promised retribution, Gunnar Yosten stepped back, breaking Noah's hold on his arm.

"Another time, then."

"Definitely."

Tamping down the adrenaline rush, Noah waited until Yosten was back on the porch before he called out, "You can leave the house keys in the mailbox. I'll pick them up when I come back."

Yosten didn't turn around to acknowledge his words. Noah spotted Barry Fairvale watching the exchange through the living room window.

Adrenaline still fired his blood when Yosten disappeared inside and he could finally stroll across the grass to Sydney's car. He half expected the sound of a shot, but nothing happened as he slid inside the car and saw Sydney's shattered expression.

"Hey." He laid his hand against her cheek. "Are you okay?"

"Who are those men?"

"The blond one said he was Gunnar Yosten."

"Laura's Gunnar?"

"You don't know him?"

Sydney shook her head. Her troubled stare remained glued to the house. "Laura and Jerome talked about him, but we've never met. No wonder Laura didn't want to go out with him. I thought the two of you were going to come to blows."

"For a minute there, so did I." Noah sat back. "He wanted to come and talk to you."

Sydney gave an involuntary shudder. "Why? What are they doing here, Noah?"

"They claim Jerome hired them to do repairs. I gather you don't know anything about that?"

"No."

"According to Fairvale, you and Jerome were going to move here."

Her mouth opened, then snapped shut. She started to say something when her attention passed him through the windshield. A police car was silently approaching. The officer cranked down his window as he pulled to a stop beside Noah's open door. "Everything okay here?"

Noah stepped from the car. "I'm Noah Inglewood." He nodded toward the house wondering which one of the neighbors had called the police. "My brother and I were co-owners of this property."

"May I see some identification?"

Slowly, Noah reached for his wallet and flipped it open. Both his military ID and his driver's license were on top.

The officer nodded quick acceptance. "Officer Jackstone." He looked toward the car expectantly.

"My brother's wife, Sydney. We came out to look at the house. We weren't aware that Jerome had hired Yosten to make any repairs. Sydney and I came up here for a little peace and quiet so I've asked Mr. Yosten and his crew to call it a day."

Officer Jackstone was a sharp young man. He sent a glance toward the house and offered a brief nod of understanding. "Would you like me to hang around for a few minutes and make sure everything is okay?"

"Yes, thank you. I'm going to take Sydney over to see Dr. Martin and grab a bite to eat. Then we'll be back."

"The Perrywrinkle is pretty decent if you don't want to travel far."

"The Perrywrinkle?"

"The old Perry place. New guy in town bought the estate and turned it into a pretty decent restaurant and bar. They do a mean steak and lobster."

"Thanks. Would you mind collecting the house keys from Mr. Yosten for me?" Their eyes met in another moment of understanding.

"No problem. Are you coming back here after dinner? I could drop them off around eight-thirty."

"Thank you. We'll be here."

"Happy to be of help, Major Inglewood."

As Noah climbed back inside the car, the police cruiser turned up the driveway. Sydney waited expectantly.

"What was that all about?"

"I'm not sure, but I get the feeling the local police share my unease about Gunnar Yosten and his crew. Officer Jackstone is going to stick around and collect the house keys for me."

"Good thinking."

He started the car. "Glad you approve."

Sydney replaced her seat belt and settled back in her seat. "Where are we going now?"

"I thought we'd stop by Doc Martin's and see if she's in. She can take a quick look at your hand and be sure you didn't do any more damage this morning."

Sydney stiffened. "I'm quite capable of selecting my own doctors, Noah."

"Hey, I know that. But you'll like Les. She and I went to school together. Besides, she's the only game in town since her father passed away."

"I don't think so."

He drove around the corner and pulled into the small lot at the side of Leslie's home office. "I was also thinking of the baby, Sydney. After what happened last night and this morning, I thought you'd want to make sure everything is okay."

Her hand automatically went to her stomach in a protective gesture. "Everything's fine."

"Sydney, will you humor me? Les is a nice lady. She won't hurt you."

"I'm sure she won't, especially since I have no intention of letting her look at me."

He turned off the engine and released his seat belt. She sat rigidly beside him. Noah sighed. "I'm issuing orders again, aren't I?"

"So it would appear."

"I apologize. I'm concerned for your welfare, Sydney. Like it or not, your body is carrying…" He hesitated over his choice of words and she jumped in to fill the gap.

"The last of your family line. Yes, I know."

This time the sarcasm surprised him. "Don't you want the baby, Sydney?"

Noah held his breath. Her answer was critical—to both of them.

"Wanting a family is what drew Jerome and me together in the first place," she said, twisting her wedding rings around and around on her finger. "But this isn't...this isn't how I thought things would go."

Noah waited, sensing the tightrope of emotions she walked.

"Jerome and I were having problems. I won't go into details since they don't matter anymore, but Jerome had this doctor friend. He'd just opened a fertility clinic outside Frederick and we...well, Jerome practically demanded we use him. I didn't like the man, and he told us the procedure didn't work. I wasn't supposed to be pregnant, Noah."

"The doctor told you this? That it didn't take?"

"That's what he said. But the surgeon at the hospital says I am pregnant and that's the only way it could have happened."

She lifted her chin defiantly, daring him to contradict her. Noah had no intention of doing so, but he wondered about that statement. Did she mean it literally, or in the sense that she didn't play around on her husband?

"All the more reason to go in and see Leslie," he told her.

"Excuse me, but I think it's all the more reason *not* to see another doctor I know nothing about."

Noah scowled. "This is hardly the same thing, Syd. The hospital didn't make a mistake."

"I know that."

She was feeling backed into a corner, he realized. An independent woman, Sydney didn't like others making her choices. He couldn't blame her.

"Okay, so what do you want to do? Do you have another doctor? One that you want to go and see?"

Sydney shook her head.

"Leslie's dad was the only doctor in Fools Point when I grew up. I have no idea how good a doctor she is, but if it means anything, Les was serious and dedicated even in high school."

"That's not exactly reassuring, Noah."

"I only suggested this because you look so tired. I thought having a local doctor take a look might be reassuring after everything that's happened, but it's your body, your decision. We could drive up to Frederick and have someone look you over if you want."

Sydney sighed. She hadn't meant to sound so ungrateful. Noah wasn't Jerome. He probably couldn't help his take-charge attitude. He wasn't really demanding, only suggesting. What could it hurt to go in and give this woman a try?

"You never answered my question, you know," Noah said.

"What question is that?"

"Do you want the baby?"

His tension told her how much her answer mattered to him. Of course it did. She was going to be the mother of his only living relative. Having this baby would tie them irrevocably together. She wasn't sure she was ready for meaningful ties to Noah Inglewood, but there really wasn't any choice.

"Of course I want my baby." And he was the second person to question that. How could anyone think she wouldn't want her own child? Were they worried she wouldn't be able to support a child?

"If my hand doesn't heal and I can't manage with just

my left, I'll find another career.'' She tried for a negligent shrug. She would not think about that possibility.

Noah shook his head impatiently. ''Your hand's going to heal, Sydney. And I plan to see that the two of you are taken care of.''

''I don't need anyone to 'take care' of me,'' she snapped. ''I'll manage. I'm quite good at taking care of myself.''

''It won't just be yourself anymore, Sydney.''

She knew. The idea was terrifying. It was also exhilarating. ''I've always wanted children.''

He sat back looking strangely pleased. ''Okay then.''

''Okay, what?''

''I think you ought to give Leslie a try.'' He held up a hand as she automatically began to protest. ''Or some other doctor. You pick, but you should know that your eyes are all squinty like you're in pain. You have very expressive eyes, Sydney. I don't want to see you in pain if there's something you can do.''

She found herself absurdly pleased that Noah cared enough to notice her eyes. Of course, he was simply looking out for his niece or nephew. Still…

Sydney stared at the doctor's large frame house. She hadn't gone inside the day Jerome had stopped by to pick up something he needed before they drove on to the clinic, so she'd never met Dr. Martin. Technically, it wasn't fair to judge the woman just because Sydney hadn't liked the other doctor Jerome had selected.

''She won't see us without an appointment.''

Noah opened the car door. ''Want to bet?''

''Noah, this isn't the military. You can't ride roughshod over a doctor.''

He smiled. She just couldn't get over the transformation of his face each time he did that.

"This is a small town," he said. "They do things differently here. But if she says no, we'll make an appointment and come back. There are only a couple of cars here right now."

"There's only room for a couple of cars," Sydney rejoined. But Noah didn't hear her. He was already coming around to the passenger side to let her out. Sydney sighed. He meant well. Of course, that was what she'd told herself about Jerome.

Sydney let Noah help her from the car, partially relieved that the decision was made. She *was* tired. And her head did hurt. So did her hand.

The receptionist looked up as they entered. Long, ebony hair drifted down her back like a cloud of silk. She had a natural, exotic beauty that was nothing short of breathtaking. When she looked up at their entrance, incredible blue-green eyes stared at them in question. Sydney checked Noah's reaction to the woman and saw only surprise on his face.

"Jasmine?" Noah asked.

The receptionist smiled pleasantly, looking vaguely puzzled. "Yes?"

"Noah Inglewood."

"Noah! Oh my gosh, I didn't recognize you." She glanced from him to Sydney, obviously pairing the two of them in her mind while taking in Sydney's somewhat battered condition curiously.

"That's hardly surprising. The last time I saw you would have been about fifteen years ago."

The young woman smiled radiantly. "I'd have been what, thirteen? I'm amazed you even recognized me after all this time."

"Hey, you were gorgeous even as a gawky teenager—which I definitely had no business noticing back then.

Besides, you have your Dad's smile. He still coaching these days?''

She flashed another wide smile. "Oh, yes. He swears he's going to retire every year, but Mom says it'll never happen." She waved her hand and smiled at Sydney to include her in the conversation. A large diamond engagement ring sparkled on one finger. Ridiculously, that symbol made Sydney relax.

"I was sorry to hear about Jerome," Jasmine was saying. "Have you been back to the house?"

Noah nodded. "We just came from there. Look, I know Leslie isn't expecting us, but I was wondering if we could see her for a few minutes."

Jasmine's glance fell sympathetically on Sydney.

"She's in with Clyde Newby right now and little Mickey Banks is waiting." Jasmine glanced at an antique wall clock. "And she's supposed to close at five." It was already seven minutes after.

"That's okay," Sydney offered. "We can make an appointment and come back."

Jasmine flashed her one of those brilliant smiles. "Is this an emergency?"

"Definitely not," Sydney said firmly.

"Well, let me at least go tell her you're out here."

Noah stopped Jasmine by simply focusing his attention on her. Sydney had a feeling that technique would probably work on most women—including herself if she wasn't careful. She was already having difficulty maintaining an emotional distance from Noah.

"Thanks, Jasmine. If she has the time, would you ask if I can speak to her a minute alone first?"

Bitter disappointment burned right through Sydney. So he was like Jerome after all, needing to be in control, trying to dominate her life. What had she expected? "I can speak to the doctor for myself, Noah."

Jasmine blinked. "Uh, let me go check with Leslie."

Sydney pushed a finger into the rock wall of his chest. "Don't you dare presume to speak for me, Noah. Not ever. If you want to give orders, go back to your unit. I am not in the military and I am not under your command and you have no rights whatsoever where I'm concerned. Is that understood?"

Though she'd tried to keep her voice down, the mother and child sitting in the waiting area watched her curiously. The door at the end of the hall opened and someone started out. She'd always hated being the focus of strangers' attention, but she would never again let another man treat her like some sort of possession.

Especially not Jerome's brother.

Giving his chest a hard shove with the heel of her hand, she turned and strode back outside, letting the screen door slam behind her. She was shaking from head to toe. Where had these blasted tears come from? She never used to cry!

"I get the feeling an apology isn't going to cut it here," Noah said quietly at her back. He came outside with barely a sound. "But I'm sorry to have upset you all the same, Syd."

"I'm going home," she said without turning around.

She could feel him weighing his response to that.

"You'll need the car keys," he finally said in that same quiet tone. "Jerome really did a number on you, didn't he?"

She whirled, wiping tears from her cheeks. "What—?"

"He was a spoiled selfish child who only got worse after Dad died. Jerome always liked things his own way.

He knew how to use his charm and good looks to get what he wanted. When I heard he married, my first thought was, that poor girl. But I assumed he'd pick a flashy spoiled type like himself, not someone like you.''

She didn't know what to say. Noah had just defined his brother's character exactly. And Noah looked genuinely contrite. She had to remind herself that Jerome had often looked contrite as well when she first started standing up to him.

"I'd like my car keys, Major.''

Without hesitation, he pulled them from his pocket and dropped them into her hand. "Planning to leave me stranded here without a car?''

His half smile was almost sad. She steeled her heart against that look.

"If it means anything,'' he continued, "I have something I personally need to ask Les about.''

"I thought military men used military doctors.''

"We do.''

Sydney waited. Noah offered no further explanation.

"You know, I really hate it when you do that,'' she told him.

"Do what?''

"Go all cryptic.''

The door opened and a wizened man with a gap-toothed smile stepped out. "Hello there, young Noah.''

Sydney stepped to the side. Young Noah? Well, perhaps from this man's perspective. He could have been anywhere from sixty to a hundred.

"Hello, Clyde. How are you?''

Clyde grunted as they shook hands, then he nodded in Sydney's direction. "Better than you, boy. Better than you. You're gonna have your work cut out for you with this one, yes indeedy. This one's got a mind of her own.''

He chortled as he turned and walked leisurely toward Main Street, his bent frame moving with surprising agility.

Noah scratched the back of his head a bit sheepishly. "Clyde is something of a Fools Point legend. He owns and runs the only movie theater in town. He and Lyle have been together ever since I can remember."

"Lyle?"

Noah shrugged. "Nobody ever knew for sure if they were 'that way' or not, but the two of them are a fixture around here. Lyle runs the gas station."

The screen door opened again and Jasmine stuck her head out. "Les will see you both in about ten minutes. I've gotta run. I left two forms on the desk. If you'd just fill them in and leave them for me, I'll make up your files tomorrow morning."

"Thanks, Jasmine," Noah began, "but there's been a change of plans."

"I'll see they're left on your desk," Sydney cut in, surprising herself as much as Noah. She walked back inside and took a seat in the empty waiting room.

Noah came in and sat beside her without saying a word. The room was empty now, but he'd chosen the seat right next to hers. Close enough that their arms bumped and she could smell his light cologne, could feel the heat of his body.

Blast it, he could make her feel angry in one heartbeat, and safe in another. But no matter what else he made her feel, her attraction to him never seemed to abate. On a purely physical level she wanted him. It was maddening.

"Noah, I'm sorry I jumped down your throat. You've been nothing but kind and I'm…"

"Rightfully stressed," he said quietly.

"That's no reason for me to be a shrew."

He gave her one of those devastating smiles. "Have you ever seen one?"

"What?"

"A shrew."

His smile was definitely the most dangerous weapon in his arsenal. Sydney found her anxiety draining away, only to be replaced by a whole other sort of tension as she regarded his mouth. What would it be like to kiss him?

"Ugly little animals, shrews," he offered. "I saw one in a zoo in Germany once. Trust me, you two look nothing alike. Maybe you're a little short-tempered, but I can deal with that."

She found herself suddenly smiling back. "Have a thing for zoos, do you? How about dealing with someone who's a lot short-tempered?"

"No, ma'am. I am not risking my neck on an opening like that one."

"You were right, you know. Your brother was charming. I didn't see the other side until after we were married."

His fingers sought hers. Warm. Offering comfort. Jerome's charm paled in comparison to Noah's. She found herself wanting to tell him everything. How Jerome had gradually changed into a person she didn't like at all.

"We didn't have a normal marriage, Noah. We were friends who wanted to have a child and create a family unit. But we weren't…we didn't really understand each other at all. What I took for protectiveness turned out to be possessiveness. Instead of making requests, he started giving orders."

"I give orders, too, but I'm not Jerome." He stared at her, willing her to understand the difference.

"I know you aren't."

Satisfied, he broke the contact and stood. "We'd better fill out those forms Jasmine left for us."

"She's very pretty." Sydney could have bitten off her tongue, but Noah didn't even blink.

"She's gorgeous. You ought to see the rest of her family. There isn't a single ugly duckling in the lot. Her brother Garrett was in my graduating class. All the women wanted to know which college he was attending."

He launched into a couple of stories until the woman and her child left the examining room accompanied by a quiet, friendly, professional woman who inspired instant confidence.

"Noah, you can come back now."

Noah didn't move. Instead, he looked at Sydney.

"Go ahead," she said.

"You sure?"

"I'm sure."

Forty minutes later, Sydney left the examining room feeling relieved for the first time since she woke up in the hospital. The doctor had seemed a little upset after her private conversation with Noah, which made Sydney more curious than ever, but she couldn't exactly ask questions about Noah's private business.

"I wish I could tell you something really encouraging about your hand, Sydney, but this sort of nerve and tissue damage is beyond my training. From what I can see on the X rays I took, your surgeon was every bit as talented as he thought he was." The women shared a smile. "I think you'll like the specialist I recommended though. The wound appears to be healing nicely and I know a couple of real good therapists I can also recommend when the time comes."

"And the baby?"

The doctor frowned. "As I said, babies are resilient.

Everything looks fine. A few bumps and bruises won't jar this little one loose, but I want you to start this vitamin supplement right away and let me know if you want the name of a good OB. Continue using the ibuprofen for your headache and pain as needed. Are you certain you don't want something a little stronger?"

"No. I'm coping pretty well. Hopefully, the worst is over. Even the vertigo seems to be more infrequent."

"Good. You're definitely on the mend."

Noah stood in the waiting room. He wasn't pacing. Sydney couldn't imagine him ever giving in to such wasted motion, but he turned from the window and watched them approach with a concerned expression.

"Everything okay?"

"Mother and child are fine. I assume you're going to keep Sydney out of harm's way for a while?"

"That's my plan. Thanks, Les."

"Leslie."

The doctor's firm correction made Sydney smile in sympathy. "Noah likes to keep everything economical, even names," Sydney told her. They shared another smile.

Noah took an affronted pose. "Oh, that's great. Gang up on me, why don't you?"

"Not a bad idea. I suspect it's the only way to get the upper hand. What do I owe you, Dr. Martin?"

Noah started to speak and quickly closed his mouth again. The doctor observed their silent exchange with obvious amusement.

"Jasmine's gone for the day," Leslie said. "Normally we bill your insurance company. If there's any problem, I have your phone number and address."

"We're going to stay at the house for the next day or so," Noah interrupted.

"Fine. Any problems or concerns, give me a call, Sydney."

"Thank you."

"Yeah, thanks, Les…lie. Hey, I'm trainable."

The doctor gave him a skeptical look. "Dobermans are easier."

Sydney chuckled. She was still grinning as they walked back outside and over to her car.

"Are you up to driving?" Noah asked.

She shook her head and handed him the keys.

"Hungry?"

"Picture that infamously overweight cartoon cat on a diet."

"That hungry, huh? Then let's try the Perrywrinkle. It's right across the street and Officer Jackstone recommended it."

"Fine with me, but the service better be fast or the tablecloth will be in jeopardy. What about the house? Do you think those men are gone?"

"They'd better be," Noah said grimly.

The Perrywrinkle was a restored mansion whose large rooms had been gutted and refitted, forming warm, cozy areas. While the restaurant was surprisingly crowded, they were seated right away. The service proved impeccable. As soon as Sydney bit into the first flaky roll, she understood the crowd. Good food, good service and a degree of intimacy not usually found in restaurants anymore.

Noah watched her devour two rolls, his eyes crinkling with humor.

"I told you I was hungry," she said defensively, reaching for a third roll.

"No problem. We can always order more."

She relaxed under his easy smile. "You should smile more often."

"I'm a major. We aren't allowed to smile. It scares the enlisted men."

Noah was so easy to like. "Why aren't you married and raising your own family?"

His amusement faded. He lifted the last roll and began to butter it. Once again she was drawn to his hands. Steady, graceful hands with neatly trimmed nails. They were working hands, all the same. She noticed a callus on his index finger.

"I am married, Sydney. To my career. I command a Special Forces unit. We can be called up at any time on a moment's notice. When that happens, we drop everything and go, no matter what. It doesn't matter if it's your kid's birthday or a wedding anniversary where you have tickets to Hawaii. We go. Not too many families cope well with that."

She mentally substituted women for families and then decided his choice was probably just as correct. No wonder he was so concerned about her baby. Obviously, he had no plans to create his own family, although she suspected he'd make a wonderful father. Depressed, she swallowed another bite of roll.

A tall, dark-haired man moved unobtrusively through the rooms, pausing at tables every so often to greet a guest. Noah came to attention without really moving. Sydney would have sworn they communicated in that split second, but both men looked away without showing the slightest trace of recognition.

"Do you know him?" she asked.

"No, but I heard someone call him Jake," Noah answered. "I think he's the owner here."

"I thought maybe you two knew each other."

His face had no readable expression. "Officer Jack-

stone said he was new in town. I've been away so long,
I barely recognize the people I used to know.''

"Good evening. Welcome to the Perrywrinkle.'' The
man appeared beside their table. His silent approach startled her so much she jumped. "Sorry. I didn't mean to
startle you. I'm Jake Collins. Is everything to your satis-
faction?''

Sydney watched the men's impersonal exchange and
wondered at the undercurrent she sensed between them.
Jake Collins was a good-looking, quietly aloof man who
carried himself with the same military precision she'd noticed in Noah.

"The food is wonderful,'' Sydney told him honestly.
"I don't know who your chef is, but he's a keeper. These
rolls are fabulous.''

Amusement muted Jake Collins's stern expression.
"I'm glad you think so. Enjoy your evening.''

"We are. Thank you.''

Noah nodded politely. Jake Collins turned away with
an almost feline economy of motion that once again reminded her of Noah.

"I wonder if he's retired Army.''

"What makes you ask that?''

"He moves like you do. No wasted effort.''

"Thanks. I think. For your information, Les…lie told
me the town thinks he's with the Mafia.''

Sydney nearly choked on a swallow of water. She set
down her glass and laughed out loud. "You're joking,
right?''

"That's what she says. He appeared out of nowhere,
bought this place and started renovations. Perfect fodder
for the gossip mill in Fools Point.''

"What do they say about me?''

His lips turned up. "I'll let you know tomorrow. By then we should be news all over town."

"I thought the purpose of coming here was to keep a low profile."

"From the bad guys. Don't worry. The townspeople don't talk to outsiders."

"I hate to point this out to you, but I've only been in town a matter of hours. I think I qualify."

His eyes smiled. "Ah, but you married a hometown boy. That puts you on the protected list."

"I see."

"Want some dessert?"

"I'd love some dessert. They have coconut cake on the menu, but I don't have any more room at the moment."

"We'll get it to go."

Before she could object, he placed an order with their unobtrusive waiter for a slice of cake and a slice of pecan pie to go. She had to remember she was dealing with a decisive military sort.

"Good timing," Noah said with a glance at his watch. "We should beat Officer Jackstone back to the house by just enough to bring your suitcase inside and turn on the lights."

Sidney felt a tremor of unease at the thought of going back to the house after that earlier scene. She was glad the policeman was meeting them there.

The sun had vanished completely, leaving a hot, muggy evening behind. She longed for a shower, but a yawn caught her almost before she could complete the thought.

"Tired?"

"Exhausted. The doctor assures me this is normal for pregnant women."

His eyes skated down her form, making her vividly

aware of her body. "We'll be at the house in just a minute."

Since the house was in walking distance, he didn't exaggerate. That was good because she'd become much too aware of Noah in a way that was very unnerving.

They turned onto the court and Sydney marveled at how dark the street was. The streetlights were far enough apart that they failed to dim the stars beaming brilliantly overhead.

Noah turned the car into the driveway and the headlights illuminated a vehicle already sitting there.

Sydney tensed, her relaxed calm instantly shattered. Visions of Noah facing down those three toughs in the front yard had her gripping the armrest.

"Scrunch down," Noah said. "Press the lock as soon as I get out of the car and drive back to the restaurant—"

"No. Wait! That's Laura's car!"

Noah froze. "Laura Gooding? Are you sure?"

"Positive. That's her license plate."

"While you were in with Leslie, I called her apartment and left a message on the answering machine to let her know where we were staying, but I never thought she'd come up here."

Noah sat still, scanning the dark area. No lights showed in his house or the ones on either side.

"Something must be wrong," she told him.

"Why don't you wait here?"

"I'd rather come with you."

Noah didn't argue as he stepped from the car, his long stride carrying him quickly to the small green compact. Sydney hurried after him.

Noah came to a sharp stop. "Get back in the car."

Frissons of fear raced through her. "What's wrong?"

"She's not inside."

"Maybe she went around to the back."

He came forward, standing so close they were practically touching. Sydney realized he was shielding her as much as possible with his body and that really frightened her. The darkness of the night suddenly concealed all sorts of hidden dangers.

"Get in the car, Syd. Please."

The please was added as an afterthought, but Sydney didn't care. His tone was low and soft and all the more scary for those very reasons. She turned to obey when they both heard a low moan.

Noah shoved her against the car and spun around. A tiny, bright flash of light appeared in his hand, aimed at the bushes. Abruptly, he headed in that direction.

Sydney's eyes took longer to make sense of what they saw in the small bright circle. Someone lay in a crumpled heap on the ground beside the porch.

Chapter Six

"Oh God, it's Laura."

Her face was bruised and cut and she whimpered when Noah touched her. Envelopes, magazines and other mail lay scattered around her.

Headlights swept up the long driveway, blinding Sydney. Noah yanked her down beside him and stood protectively over her, all in one blur of motion. He relaxed just as quickly.

"Jackstone! Call for an ambulance!"

Noah obviously had far better night vision than she did. Only when the car door opened did Sydney realize it was a police car.

The next several minutes passed in a haze of activity. The police officer radioed for backup and an ambulance while Sydney crooned to her friend, vainly offering words of meaningless comfort, unsure whether Laura could hear her or not.

Horror and fear gnawed at her stomach. The ambulance crew arrived in minutes and she found herself waiting impatiently inside the police car while Noah and another officer searched the grounds and then the house for whoever had assaulted her friend. And all the while, guilt built inside her.

Dry-eyed, she watched Noah and Jackstone return to the vehicle. "You doing okay?" Noah demanded.

She nodded, feeling detached and scared all at the same time.

"Sydney," Jackstone said kindly, "do you know of anyone who would hurt your friend like this?"

Sydney shook her head and tried not to shiver. "No one."

"No jilted lovers, ex-boyfriends?"

Her gaze flicked to Noah.

"I told him about Yosten."

"But she never even went out with him."

"He was here today," Noah reminded her.

Sydney wrapped her good arm protectively against her body.

"No one else, Sydney?" Jackstone asked.

Sydney shook her head. "Laura has a lot of friends, but she isn't dating anyone special right now."

"Okay." He turned to Noah. "Why don't you follow me to the hospital. Maybe Laura can give me a statement."

But Laura wouldn't be giving any statements that evening. Her jaw had been broken and the doctors had rushed her into surgery to repair the damage. They waited until Laura was in the recovery room and the doctor assured them that no permanent damage had been done. Laura would sleep until morning, but she'd make a complete recovery. Noah thanked the doctor and then drove the two of them to a nearby motel.

Sydney was thankful for his silent presence. His frequent light touches while they waited had been a comforting communication worth more than idle words. A sort of "I'm here, you're not alone" reassurance that calmed the demons inside her.

Sydney knew he'd planned on spending the night at the house, but she was glad when he chose a motel instead. Maybe it was cowardly, but an impersonal motel felt safer than that large unknown house with its multiple ways in and out.

By the time they checked in, she could barely keep her eyes open—until they reached the room. Room singular. There were two double beds, no connecting door.

She raised her eyes in silent question.

"I'm not leaving you alone tonight, Sydney. Not until we know who attacked Laura and what she was doing in Fools Point."

The set of his features told her he was braced for an argument. She didn't have that sort of energy left. Besides, she wasn't sure she wanted to argue. After last night, sleeping alone in a strange room would have been terrifying.

Sydney headed straight for the bathroom. When she returned, she found Noah had set her suitcase on one of the beds and spread it open for her.

"Turn around, Syd."

"What for?"

"So I can undo your zipper."

Her stomach gave an unexpected flip. Until now, she'd been trying not to think of the two of them together in this small room all night. But the thought of his hands removing her dress started a quivery sensation low in her belly. It would be safer to tell him she could do it herself—but it would have been a lie.

"Turn around," he said again.

A moment ago, she'd been certain she barely had the energy to fall into bed. Leave it to her hormones to send out a wake-up call.

Noah apparently decided she was unable to comprehend his direction. Gently, but firmly, he turned her around with a swift economy of motion. Sydney desperately tried to contain a tremor of physical excitement. Tingles coursed through her body at the touch of his broad hands. A sweep of heat stirred low in her belly, powerfully exhilarating.

She told herself that she was grateful Noah could be so impersonal. But that was a lie, too. A foolish, feminine part of her wanted this arrangement to bother Noah as much as it did her. His fingertips brushed her bare skin, making her shiver. Did his hands linger a bit longer than necessary or was that her highly charged imagination at work?

"Do you want help getting into a nightgown?"

His voice was so calm, so unaffected. She should have been glad. She didn't want him interested in her in a sensual way. Did she?

A tiny voice cried, *Yes.*

"Sydney? Is something wrong?"

"Yes." Desire was sliding along her nerve endings like tiny flashes of electricity. She twisted to face him. "I'm not some mannequin you offered to dress and undress."

His mouth opened to protest, but the words were never uttered. His gaze was snagged by the expanse of bare skin revealed as the dress slipped down her shoulder. The air practically crackled as he lifted his gaze to hers.

Noah wasn't as uninterested as he pretended.

"I prefer sleeping nude," she said quietly. His eyes darkened, absorbing her words, and she added, "Like you."

Noah cleared his throat. "Uh, for tonight, I think we'd both better make an exception." He reached out to tug at the drooping shoulder and his knuckles brushed her bare shoulder. He froze. So did she.

''I'll let you finish while I use the bathroom,'' he said abruptly.

Sydney watched his precise, military pivot with a combination of relief, amusement and dejection. Face it. She was wickedly attracted to Noah, whether she should be or not. Maybe she could blame it all on hormones. The doctor had said a woman's hormones changed during pregnancy.

''Sydney?'' His voice was only slightly muffled by the bathroom door. ''You're nothing like a mannequin.''

Ridiculously, she found herself smiling. The smile became a grin that widened as she began searching for a nightgown. She selected one at random and worked the dress down and off one-handed. The nightgown's nylon material proved slippery, but she finally managed to pull it on.

She loved sexy, frilly personal garments, but a glance in the mirror over the dresser gave her pause. Had she chosen this particular gown subconsciously because she *wanted* Noah to notice her? The fitted bodice cupped her breasts, while the silky peach nylon molded itself to her body.

No. Attracting men had never been a priority with her. Her first instinct was to take the gown off and find something a little less provocative, but all her gowns were a similar style. Hadn't Noah made it abundantly clear that while he might find her attractive, he wasn't lusting after her? She climbed into the empty bed and was struggling to pull up the covers when Noah returned.

''Here. I'll get them.''

She'd been right. The gown didn't disturb him a bit. It was enough to make a woman grit her teeth. Noah wore jogging shorts and a T-shirt that emphasized his strong legs and well-honed body.

Must be hormones, she decided. Finding him attractive was bad enough. Lusting after his body was insane.

"I'll tuck you in," Noah offered. His hair was damp and he smelled so good she could have lain there and drunk in the scent of him forever. She really was losing it. Thank heavens Noah was back in his detached mode. She should be glad one of them was being sensible.

But she wasn't.

In the act of stepping back, Noah surprised them both by reaching down to tenderly brush the hair back from her face. Sydney trembled. His eyes deepened with intensity. The air practically crackled between them.

"You could use another aspirin, I think," he said finally.

"I...took some ibuprofen in the bathroom." She shut her eyes to avoid looking at him while the wanting hammered at her soul. Now that she had his attention, she wasn't sure what to do with it. "I'm just tired." A great excuse for idiocy.

"I know."

The compassion in his voice snapped her eyes open. "Noah?"

Impulsively, she reached for his hand.

Touching him was a big mistake. She was too needy tonight, and his fingers were warm, imparting strength where they clasped hers.

"What was Laura doing there?" Sydney managed to ask.

Noah knew Sydney probably blamed herself for what had happened to her friend, but if there was any guilt to assign it was his. He should have thought to protect Laura better after someone tore up her apartment. He shouldn't have left that message on the answering machine where anyone could have found it and played it back.

"There was mail on the ground, Sydney. Yours and Jerome's."

Stricken, Sydney stared at him. "She said she'd check the apartment mail for me."

"And I left her a message on the answering machine telling her where we were so she wouldn't worry."

"I meant to call her myself, Noah. I just forgot with everything that's been happening. Why did she come here tonight?"

"We'll have to wait until she can tell us." But he'd had several thoughts along that line, all of which he'd shared with the police and the FBI during the long wait at the hospital.

"We look a lot alike," Sydney said quietly. "Especially in the dark. We both have long brown hair."

Noah wished she hadn't made that particular connection, but he wasn't surprised. Sydney was an intelligent woman. "I told Agent Wickowski about the men who were at the house today."

"I didn't see him at the hospital."

She rose on her elbow, causing the blanket to dip. The smooth expanse of her upper chest lay enticingly exposed, plunging to the deep vee of her bodice. His gaze skated over the view, wanting to stop and linger.

"He wasn't at the hospital. I called him when I went to get you that fruit juice. Wickowski knows his job, Sydney. If there's a connection, he or the police will find it."

"There was no reason for anyone to hurt Laura."

The pain in her voice reached inside him, stirring his guilt. He sat beside her on the bed. The mattress sank, causing her to roll toward him, against his hip. She had such wide, expressive eyes. He wanted to remove the pain that lingered there, but all he could do was stroke her cheek with the back of a knuckle while his own chest tightened with suppressed emotion.

"They thought she was me, didn't they?"

"I don't know."

But he could guess. And that guess had been troubling him all evening. If any of those men *had* been involved in the robbery, finding Sydney at the house this afternoon must have come as quite a shock. Either they mistook Laura for Sydney when they caught her there alone tonight, or Laura's beating had been intended as a warning to Sydney to keep her mouth shut. Either way, Noah was firmly convinced all these events were somehow related to the bank robbery.

"There's no point speculating, Sydney," he told her gently. "We're going to have to wait until Laura can give us some information."

"I feel responsible."

"So do I." He kissed her forehead, intending to stand and move away. Sydney surprised him by reaching out, lightly touching the side of his face. Without thinking about it, he turned his face into her palm, kissing the smooth surface.

Her eyes widened, then the long silky lashes fluttered down to block them from his view. In an unconscious action, her tongue peeked out to moisten her lips.

"I lied to you," she said.

His muscles contracted. He needed to walk away right now. Because if he didn't, his brother's wife or not, he was going to give in to this attraction he'd been fighting from the start and do something stupid—like kiss those compellingly sensual lips.

"What did you lie about?"

"I said I could take care of myself. But right now—"

she swallowed hard, her expression totally defenseless
"—right now I'm very glad you're here."

He studied the curve of her cheek, surprised that he felt
as if he already knew each line and plane of her face.
Simple lust he could deal with, but looking at Sydney, he
knew none of the things he was feeling was simple.

This was Jerome's wife.

Noah realized he didn't care.

She'd said they never had a normal marriage. Jerome
was dead. Noah didn't owe his brother a thing. At least,
not where Sydney was concerned. In fact, very much the
opposite.

"I'll be here, Sydney. I'm not going anywhere." Instead of a promise, the words sounded suspiciously like a
vow.

Sydney regarded him with a banked longing he could
almost taste. Their tenuous magnetism, never far from the
surface, now lay exposed in the gaze she fastened so
raptly on his mouth. His muscles tightened. Her lips
parted in silent invitation.

His heart began beating a crazy tattoo. "Sydney?"

She raised her eyes. The slight hitch in her breathing
acted as a spur. Slowly, unable to help himself, Noah
leaned over and covered her lips with his own.

Her lips clung sweetly, incredibly soft. Her hand
clasped the back of his neck in subtle, unknowing en-
couragement. Need, insistent and forceful, seared his gut.

She made a small sound low in her throat. Her lips
parted further, inviting a deeper kiss. Noah surrendered to
the unbearable temptation to sample her mouth, touching
her tongue, exploring her inner warmth. In a heartbeat,
the kiss threatened to go all hot and wild and demanding.
Noah managed to pull back, shocked by the strength of

his desire to cover her mouth and body and taste her completely.

Far from looking offended, Sydney's expression held only poignant yearning. Arousal suffused her cheeks with enticing pink color and darkened her eyes with the same need clawing at his gut. He wanted her—and she wasn't saying no. But surrendering now to the sweetness of her unspoken invitation was to invite disaster. She'd regret it in the morning.

He'd regret it as well. There was too much between them—and not enough. *His lie was much larger than hers.*

Noah stood. She needed to know what he'd discovered today when he'd spoken with Leslie, but the words lodged in his throat.

Acceptance, understanding and maybe even gratitude flickered in her eyes. She lay back with a soft little sigh, letting her head settle more deeply into the pillow. Regret? Her vulnerable expression held no trace of reproach.

"Noah, I'm so tired. Could you...would you hold me? Just...hold me. I'll be strong tomorrow, I promise. Tonight I just need to be held. Please."

A resounding *no* formed in his head, but refused to leave his lips. There was nothing provocative in her request. She seemed to have no idea what she was asking. He hadn't expected this almost primitive need to claim her that settled deep in his gut. She looked so trusting, so incredibly tantalizing.

And he knew he was going to do as she'd asked, even though he'd be tempting fate to its limit.

"Push over."

Obediently, she shifted to make room. He tried to still the pounding of his heart, careful to keep his body outside the covers. As if she were more delicate than spun glass, he pulled her against his chest.

And all he could think was it had been a good thing he hadn't removed his shirt in the bathroom, because holding her against his bare skin would have been tempting fate one step too far. He only wished he'd added another layer of cloth. Not that any amount of clothing would act as a sufficient barrier to the energy singing through his body right now.

She nestled against him. He wanted to groan in frustration.

"Thank you."

Noah couldn't reply. The clean fragrance of her shampoo filled his head. He could feel every inch of her warm body where it pressed against his own. He should have turned the air conditioner all the way down before touching her.

It wouldn't have helped.

"You're welcome," he finally managed. He stroked her hair. Thick, silky, as tempting as the rest of her. He could feel her relaxing against him and had to shift before she noticed his body's response. It had been far too long since he'd simply held a woman this way.

Who was he kidding? He'd never held a woman this way. He couldn't remember ever *wanting* to hold a woman this way. Feelings and sensations were burrowing under his skin much deeper than mere sexual need. And that need was strong enough to scare him witless right now. He wanted to roll Sydney beneath him and do all the wanton things running through his mind.

"I know you'll find this hard to believe," she mumbled, "but I'm not usually this weak."

Weak? She thought she was weak? "You don't have to worry, Syd. I think you're one tough lady."

"Good," she muttered sleepily. "Have to be strong… to deal with a man like you."

With a sardonic smile, he rubbed his chin and jaw against her silky hair. "Go to sleep before your sweet talk goes to my head."

"We *should* talk," she murmured in agreement.

Noah stroked her bare arm. "We will. In the morning."

She mumbled something he couldn't understand. He didn't ask her to repeat it, and after a few moments she became still. Soon her breathing deepened until he knew she had slipped into sleep. He was amazed how fast she could do that. One minute awake, the next sound asleep.

Noah watched the steady rise and fall of her chest, glad he had covered that excuse for a nightgown with the blanket. Keeping his distance had become a challenge. He was starting to feel possessive where she was concerned and it scared him. Not as much as it would probably scare her if she knew.

He should get up, put her suitcase on the floor and climb into the opposite bed like a gentleman. Too bad he wasn't feeling very gentlemanly at the moment. Instead, he found himself strangely reluctant to let go of her. Sydney felt right nestled in his arms like this. Was it simply because it had been so long since he'd been with a woman?

She didn't so much as stir. He could feel her soft breath on his shirt.

"Don't worry, Syd," he whispered. "You and the baby are mine to protect. No one is going to hurt you ever again."

Sydney didn't move. Noah closed his eyes and wondered how he was going to keep that promise. But he would, or die trying.

HE WOKE, fully aroused, to the sounds of people moving in the hall outside their door. The right side of his body tingled numbly where Sydney lay half on top of him. Lights blazed inside the room, but he knew hours had passed.

He'd fallen asleep. And slept deeply, judging by how rested he felt. Sydney was still sleeping, her silky hair tumbled across him, tickling his chin and cheek. Her good hand lay on his thigh, perilously close to that part of his anatomy that had awakened first.

Talk about sweet torture.

His watch showed the time was 0700 hours. They'd slept straight through the night without moving. That explained the painful numbness. Still, he continued to ignore the prickles of discomfort in order to lie there, listening to the sound of her breathing. The need to care for her hadn't diminished any more than his need to make love to her.

That thought jolted him completely awake. Carefully, he tried to ease his way free of her embrace. She came with him and her hand covered the jutting stretch of fabric on his pants.

His heart thudded expectantly. She nuzzled his shirt. Her hand slid over his hardened ridge of flesh. Every single atom of him became hard as stone. He tried to swallow and couldn't. When he tried to move away again, her eyes fluttered open.

"Hi."

Sleep-drenched, her body was softer, more yielding and ten times more tempting.

He wanted to laugh. He wanted to curse. He was only a man.

"Hi yourself."

And he lowered his head toward those incredible lips

and fit his mouth over hers. She returned his kiss, turning more fully toward him, pressing her hand more firmly against him.

He deepened the kiss, knowing he was taking unfair advantage, but unable to stop. She responded ardently, opening beneath the pressure of his tongue to surrender her mouth.

Noah knew the exact moment when she came fully awake and realized who he was, where they were and what they were doing.

She stilled completely and her eyes flew open. Her hand drew back as if scorched. Quite possible from the heat he was generating.

Noah rolled away. He stood quickly, welcoming the fiery pinpricks of returning circulation. It helped keep his mind off the blood circulating in other parts of his body.

The covers had come dislodged and her gown had shifted, displaying most of one generous breast. Through a fabric designed to drive a man mad, he could make out the darker-colored circle where her rigid nipple lay barely hidden from view. Noah tore his gaze away before she noticed or he gave in to his strong desire for a better view and climbed right back into that bed with her.

"I'm going to grab a quick shower." Ice-cold and as punishing as he could make it.

Sydney didn't respond. When he came out of the bathroom, she was sitting on the edge of the bed clutching a pile of clothing to her chest. It didn't hide the fact that she had a very nice chest.

"How are you feeling?" he greeted.

She wouldn't meet his eyes. "Embarrassed."

"Why?"

She looked to the other bed, which had obviously not been slept in, and then at him.

Noah walked over and lifted her chin. She quivered beneath his touch. "Needing someone doesn't make you weak, Sydney."

"It can." Her eyes sparkled, proudly defiant. "I don't see you needing anyone."

"Really? Then you aren't looking close enough."

He lowered his head and captured her lips. Shock held her still the length of one heartbeat, then she jerked her head back.

"No!"

"You're right. But I'm not going to apologize, Syd."

"I don't want an apology."

"Good. Go take your shower while I try to find some liquid caffeine."

Sydney watched him leave the room while wild, impossible images tumbled through her head. He'd kissed her again.

And she'd kissed him back.

And she wanted to do a lot more than simply kiss him. The knowledge shouldn't have stunned her. Sex had never been all that important to her. Her experience had been that it never lived up to its billing.

Until Noah?

No! She would not think like that! Propinquity. That's all it had been. They were thrust together in an abnormal situation and he was an extremely sensual man. Good-looking, in that confident, sure-of-himself way that many women found irresistible. She was no exception. What she had to remember was that the kisses hadn't meant anything to him.

Still, if he had apologized she would have been mortified. She'd invited that kiss, and more besides.

The shower only brought her thoughts into sharper focus and forced her to admit the truth. Wasn't it just last night that she was upset because he hadn't even noticed she was a woman? Well, he'd noticed now. And she'd wanted him to.

Wasn't that the reason she'd been so prickly with him all along? She didn't want this wild attraction to him, but she could no longer deny the truth. At least not to herself.

She was sexually attracted to Noah and she had been right from the start. There was no use denying the attraction, but she told herself dependency played a role here. Like when a patient fell in love with her doctor.

Not that she was falling in love with Noah. It was more like lust. But she didn't *do* lust. At least she never had before Noah. No man had ever stirred her emotions like this.

Lust or love?

Did it matter? Neither one was acceptable.

She pulled on the semisheer bra that fastened in the front and after four abortive tries, finally managed to work the clasp with her good hand, while pinning the thing in place with her bad arm. She donned a loose-fitting cotton blouse and stepped into panties and a pair of shorts.

As soon as she left the bathroom, she knew Noah had found his caffeine. The smell of coffee filled the bedroom, but it had no appeal for her at all this morning. The small table near the window held coffee, but also tea, juice and bagels. And the slice of cake and the pie from the night before.

Noah had opened the drape, filling the room with natural light. Another hot, hazy day, judging from the sky. He was replacing the telephone in its cradle.

"I just spoke to Agent Wickowski. Laura is going to be fine. Her parents flew in from Kansas this morning. She's going home to stay with them for a few days."

"I'm so relieved. Her parents are wonderful people.
Did she say what happened?"

"She told her co-worker she had to pick up the new
keys to her apartment and then she was going to swing
by your place and collect the mail and the plants."

Sydney nodded, her gaze straying toward the African
violet Noah had carried in from the car last night along
with their luggage. "She offered to get them for me."

Noah's expression was grim. "Well, I'm afraid she discovered her apartment wasn't the only one the burglars
were interested in."

"They broke into Jerome's place too?"

"I'm afraid so. She called the police and, after talking
to them, decided to bring the mail and tell us in person
what had happened. She started up the porch steps and
someone ran at her out of the darkness and threw her to
the ground. I'm not going to sugarcoat it, Sydney. He
thought she was you."

"Oh, Noah."

"He was wearing a ski mask, so she never got a look
at his face. He just demanded she tell him where the tape
was."

"What tape?"

"That's the million-dollar question. Laura didn't recognize his voice so that pretty much leaves Yosten out of
things. She's sure she would have recognized him."

"It could have been one of the other two."

"Yes. Or someone we've never met. The police are
checking every possible lead."

"But what tape?"

"Could the man who attacked you also have wanted a
tape?"

"I guess. I really don't know."

He rubbed his jaw wearily. "The only tapes Wickowski

can think of are the bank's surveillance tapes. They thought the robbers took them along with the money. But even if they didn't, unless Jerome removed them and gave them to you *before* the robbery, there's no way you could have gotten them out of the bank that day.''

"Do they really think—?''

"No. Sydney, the only way this makes sense is if someone wants a tape that belonged to Jerome.''

"Fine. He has a slew of videotapes. They can have all of them. He buys…he bought a lot of old movies on tape. But he doesn't even own a video camera. There are no home movies or that sort of thing.''

"What about music tapes?''

Sydney shook her head, her thoughts racing to find a connection to Jerome and some sort of tape. "He only listens to CDs, even in his car.''

"No tape recorder?''

"Not that I've ever seen. The CD player does play tapes, but he doesn't have any that I know of.''

Noah stared into space as if his mind was somewhere else. Sydney combed her memory for any sort of tape connected with Jerome and came up blank.

But she didn't know any details about what Jerome had been doing for the past two months and that thought stopped her. He'd been spending time in Fools Point from what he'd said. She was about to tell Noah that when he spoke.

"Did Jerome ever give you a package to hold for him?''

"No.''

"A book? Anything that might contain a tape of some sort?''

"Nothing. I swear, Noah. He wasn't the sort to buy presents. Not even before we were married. I mean, he'd give a gift for a birthday or something, but…'' She shook her head. "You must know what he was like."

"Actually, I do and I don't." He hesitated for just a second. "I'm not sure if you know this or not, but Jerome was my half brother."

Her breath caught. "You weren't full brothers?"

"No. My mother died of complications due to pneumonia when I was thirteen." Remembered pain still reflected in his voice. "A year later, my father ran into a woman he'd had an affair with while my mother was still alive."

"Jerome's mother?" she guessed.

He nodded. The tight set of Noah's jaw told her how difficult the admission was for him. He'd spoken of his mother with fondness. Knowledge of his father's affair must have hurt him deeply. Especially at that impressionable age.

"Jerome was already three, and since my mother had just died, Dad decided to do the right thing by his other woman." His lack of inflection spoke more loudly than a striking denouncement. "They married right away and he brought Callie and Jerome to live with us in Fools Point. I was still reeling from my mother's unexpected death and I resented the intrusion of Callie and her son."

"You were disappointed in your father," she said softly.

He looked at her. "No, I was mad as hell. I couldn't believe my father had cheated on her that way."

There wasn't anything to say to that. Sydney remembered her own family's deaths and the sense of loss and anger and betrayal. Thirteen was a tough age anyhow.

"I'm afraid I made things pretty rough on everyone," Noah continued. "Fortunately, I played a lot of sports, which kept me busy, and Colonel Sayers, my ROTC instructor, got me interested in the military. He helped me get the ROTC scholarship."

"So you substituted the military for your family?"

Noah seemed surprised by her perception. "Yes. In a real sense, that's exactly what I did. Eventually, my dad and I came to terms. I couldn't condone his action, but I didn't hate him anymore. I even accepted Callie and Jerome, but once I graduated high school, I wasn't home much except for periodic visits."

He stared out the window. Sydney knew he was looking through the glass into his past. She waited quietly.

"Dad died in an accident on the Beltway a few years later. I'm ashamed to admit, I pretty much stopped going home after that." He ran a hand across his jaw. "I realize I should have made more of an effort with Jerome. None of it was his fault any more than it was mine. Callie was actually a nice person and I think she loved my dad. At least they seemed happy enough together, but Callie..." Noah sighed. "She didn't know how to cope very well. After Dad died, she let Jerome get away with murder."

Sydney touched his hand. "Jerome was spoiled, but he could be incredibly nice too. Even breathtakingly charming when he wanted to be," she said softly.

"And he was good-looking," Noah agreed without rancor.

"Actually, he was close to beautiful. I think that was part of the problem. Women were always coming on to him. It actually annoyed him. I was stunned when he started paying attention to me. Because he worked next door at the bank, we often took lunch breaks at the same time. When he realized this, we began taking them together. He was so attentive, I was flattered."

"Most women were. What went wrong?" Noah asked.

It was Sydney's turn to sigh. The truth was difficult.

How could she possibly explain going into a sexless, love-less marriage with his brother? In hindsight, she found it difficult to understand herself. Just because sex had never played an important part in her life seemed like such a stupid reason to agree to a lifetime commitment.

Noah regarded her steadily.

"We became friends who shared a common dream."

He frowned. "Having a child?"

She couldn't quite meet his eyes. "Yes. Having a family was important to both of us. Too much so, as it turned out. We didn't really know each other all that well. After a while, I realized we'd rushed into marriage and made a mistake." A huge, life-shattering mistake. But Noah didn't need details of her stupidity.

"Jerome could be demanding."

"Oh, yes. I should have seen that sooner. *Don't wear your hair like that. That dress makes you look fat. You're spending too much time with your friends.*"

Noah shifted. Sydney hesitated, unsure whether to continue or not. "I guess it all sounds petty now, but it didn't feel that way at the time."

"You're an independent woman. Frankly, I'm surprised he'd have the nerve to tell you what to wear." Noah's smile took the sting from his words.

"Don't get the wrong impression. Our problems weren't all one-sided. Relationships never are. The problem was, we stopped being able to communicate."

"It happens."

She shook her head. "I should probably have tried harder. After I left the apartment and moved back in with Laura and Hannah, Jerome started coming around at lunchtime. We'd hold these whispered arguments so no one would overhear."

She swallowed down the painful memories. "He

wouldn't accept my decision. He actually ordered me to move back to the apartment.''

Silently, she bit back the rest.

"Did he threaten you, Syd?"

"Once," she admitted reluctantly. "That's when I finally called a lawyer."

She stood abruptly. "I don't want to talk about this, Noah. Jerome is dead. Let's go check out your house. I know he came up here during the past few weeks. Maybe he left a tape at the house."

SYDNEY WAS OBVIOUSLY embarrassed by what she'd revealed, but none of it surprised him. What did, Noah acknowledged to himself, was the fact that his brother was a complete idiot. How could he marry someone like Sydney and not cherish her?

He'd been putting off his own embarrassing truth long enough. It had been obvious from his first conversation with Sydney in the hospital, that she had no idea just how devious and controlling Jerome really was. He'd wanted to tell her then and there, but she'd already had so many shocks that the timing never seemed right. Now, he worried that he'd left it until too late.

The big old house stood silently welcoming in the hazy bright sun. In spite of what had happened to Laura out front, the house held a lot of memories for Noah—most of them good. Sydney looked sadly at the small signs of the disturbance from the night before while he unlocked the front door.

"Come on. Try not to think about it."

She didn't answer, but stepped inside the large old foyer quickly and stared around.

"Big rooms."

"Yeah. There was always plenty of space for friends to come over and play."

"What's behind that door on the stair landing?"

Her finger pointed up the front stairs to the small landing where the steps took a right-hand jog before continuing on up.

"Another set of stairs come up from the kitchen—a sort of servants' staircase. As kids, we loved running up and down those steps, but I think the real purpose was so servants could go upstairs without walking through the living room and interrupting conversations. The house is pretty old, Sydney."

"Oh." She turned away and peered into the room to the right. "I didn't expect it to be furnished either."

His father's den off the front foyer had been completely redone in chrome and black metal and white leather. White walls had replaced the warm, dark paneling Noah remembered. He wondered what had happened to his father's old walnut desk and matching file cabinet. And what had become of the freestanding globe his father had been so proud of? All that remained were the walnut bookcases, devoid of books.

"Some of this stuff belonged to my parents, although Callie made changes after she moved in." He stood beside Sydney in front of the entrance to the living room. "I don't remember that couch or those chairs, but the end tables and bookcases are the same." He could still see the nick on the coffee table where he'd rammed a toy truck into it.

He also noted that the chair cushion had been pulled out and put back in place upside down. Also, the bookcase had been pulled away from the wall and pushed back, not quite in the same position. Realization hit him.

Someone had been going through the house.

"I'm surprised Jerome rented the house furnished," Sydney said, obviously not seeing the signs of intrusion.

Noah set the magazine and envelope he'd retrieved from the bushes on the hall table where a pile of mail already sat. "Jerome figured it was easier to rent the house furnished." Noah took in other, small signs of invasion, unwilling to point them out to her just yet. "Turns out he was right. We never lacked for tenants."

She walked through the living room into the dining room.

"This is a fabulous old house, Noah!" Sydney said. "Look at that wainscoting!"

Noah peered around the formal dining room. He wasn't sure what wainscoting was, but he liked the expression of pleasure it brought to her face. What he didn't like seeing was the half-open drawer on the credenza where a white linen tablecloth had gotten stuck, stopping it from closing all the way.

Someone had definitely been going through the rooms. They'd just done a neater job here at the house than they'd done on Laura's apartment.

"Oh, what a beautiful kitchen!"

The bright room beckoned cheerfully.

"Callie had it gutted and redone a few years back." And he had to admit, the light oak cupboards were a big improvement over the dark ones he remembered.

Signs of habitation were plain in the kitchen, but as Noah had told the police last night, Yosten and his crew had apparently been given full run of the house. Empty beer and soda cans and crumpled bags of chips attested to the use they'd made of the kitchen, at least. There were also signs of repair here and there. A patched place on one wall, what appeared to be a new faucet on the sink.

Sydney had a funny expression on her face. Her body

had become tense as she sniffed the air. Noah sniffed as well. The scent of some spicy Italian dish lingered in the air. In the sink he discovered two dirty plates with remnants of some sort of pasta dish and a half-eaten slice of garlic bread.

"The man in the hospital and the hotel room smelled of garlic," she said softly.

"Lots of people eat garlic bread, Sydney." But he made a mental note not to touch the plate and to let Wickowski know.

"True." She looked up the back staircase. "How many bedrooms?"

"Four. All good-sized rooms. Let's go up and you can have a look around."

"Shouldn't we start searching for the tape?"

"I think it's going to prove a waste of time, Sydney. Someone's already gone through the house."

"What do you mean? How do you know?"

A floorboard creaked overhead, stopping his answer cold.

Chapter Seven

"Wait here," Noah ordered. Before she could argue, he charged up the servants' stairs from the kitchen. The footsteps overhead had already started down. Now they thundered down the front steps with no attempt at silence as the person began to run.

Noah found himself stopped at the landing. The door was locked or jammed from the other side.

Sydney ran back through the dining room, hoping to catch a glimpse of the person, but Noah overtook her, grabbing her arm and nearly scaring her to death. "Stay here!"

The front door slammed shut. Noah sprinted in that direction. Sydney followed more cautiously. The intruder was already out of sight. Leaving the front door open, Noah rushed outside and leaped over the side of the porch. He immediately disappeared from view.

Sydney leaned over the railing to watch Noah running toward the back of the neighboring house. Her impulse was to chase after them, but common sense prevailed. She'd do Noah more good by going inside and calling the police.

She hurried into the den off the foyer. The desktop was empty. Where was the telephone? She whirled to try the kitchen when a sudden noise overhead held her riveted in place.

For a moment, she wasn't sure just what she'd heard. The house was frighteningly silent. Then came the smallest of sounds. It took her a second to realize someone had just opened the door on the landing. Fear crashed through her.

The intruder hadn't been alone!

She swept the room for a hiding place. From outside came several popping sounds. Gunshots? Her gaze flew to the window. Noah!

Sydney spun, seeking a weapon. The only portable item in the entire room was the cast-iron duck doorstop. Not much use against a gun, but hefting it, she decided it would make a solid thunk if she got close enough to throw it. She pushed aside the fear that urged her to crawl under the desk. Noah was in trouble and it was up to her to help.

Peering around the corner, she had a clear view of the living room as well as the stairs. The door on the landing now stood open. That meant the second intruder had probably gone down the back stairs into the kitchen.

Her throat went dry while her heart tried to beat its way free. Every instinct shouted for her to run. But run where? Noah had the keys to the car and someone was outside shooting at him. She *had* to find a telephone and call for help.

She eyed the open front door. The gulf between the houses looked enormous. She'd be a fully exposed target as she ran. Could she make it to a neighbor's house before the gunman saw her? And what if the neighbor wasn't home? She wouldn't do Noah any good if she was dead.

An image of Noah already lying in the grass somewhere added urgency. Gripping the heavy duck doorstop as tightly as she could, she crept into the hall on legs that threatened to turn to liquid any second. The back door opened and closed quietly.

Sydney froze. She tried to remain calm, but her shaking intensified. Had the second intruder gone outside or had someone else come in? She couldn't stand here paralyzed.

If only she could remember whether there'd been a telephone on the wall near the kitchen table.

Holding the duck in a death grip, Sydney took a deep breath and crossed the hall into the living room. In the dining room she paused again, straining to hear any sound. All she could hear was the hammering of her own pulse. Was she alone in the house or not?

Sydney hated her panic almost as much as she hated her indecisiveness. And she really hated whoever these men were.

Anger acted as a catalyst. Before she could change her mind, she rushed into the kitchen, the heavy doorstop raised as a weapon.

The kitchen was empty.

She ran to the back door, set the duck on the table and threw the dead bolt. A long, ill-kept backyard swept downward toward a line of trees. They were part of the heavily wooded areas that surrounded Fools Point. She glimpsed a running figure disappearing behind one of the trees. The intruder? And if so, which one?

Where was Noah?

She scanned the area, straining to spot him. Nothing else moved. The hazy afternoon sun seared the quiet landscape. Not even a dog barked. Nature seemed to be holding its breath, waiting to see what would happen.

And a horrible thought leaped out of ambush. Noah had confronted three men at the house yesterday. Two people had already left. If they were the same men, that meant a third person could still be inside.

Her mind screamed in protest, but Sydney forced herself to turn slowly and survey the room. No telephone.

Of course there was no telephone! The last tenants would have had it disconnected when they moved. She wasn't thinking clearly or she'd have thought of this much sooner. Panic could get her killed.

Her gaze came to rest on two closed doors. One no doubt led to a basement, but the other could connect with anything from a laundry room to a pantry or a bathroom. And anyone could be on the other side of either door—or still waiting upstairs.

Fear made way for dry-mouthed terror. The memory of Laura's battered face melded with memories of her own attacks. The very silence of the house preyed on her nerves.

Sydney grabbed the cast-iron duck and ran through the dining room. She'd take her chances outside. At least there she could yell until she drew every neighbor for miles around. But as she sprinted toward the front door, a figure suddenly loomed in the opening without warning.

Sydney screamed. Too late, she recognized the figure limping inside. By then, the duck had already left her hand.

"Sydney!"

Noah dodged needlessly. The heavy piece of cast iron plummeted immediately to the floor with a harmless crash. Noah came to a shocked halt.

"What the devil...?"

"I thought...I thought you were one of them!"

Momentarily speechless, Noah stared at her. In two strides he was across the room, pulling her against his chest. She didn't resist despite his sweaty, dirt-stained clothing. She was shaking so hard her teeth were chattering.

"Are you hurt?" he demanded. "Sydney! Are you hurt?"

With a shake of her head she lifted her face. "No. I heard shots."

"He missed." Noah dismissed that completely. "You're not hurt?"

"No."

Noah drew back. "What did you mean, one of them?"

She tugged his arms and lowered her voice to whisper. "There was someone else upstairs," she told him.

Ice formed side by side with regret in his chest. He should never have left her alone.

"After you left, someone else went down the back stairs and out the back door. I threw the dead bolt, but it occurred to me that yesterday there were three men here at the house so maybe…"

He hadn't even thought about that, hadn't taken any time to wonder who he was chasing. It could have been yesterday's trio, or anyone else for that matter. He should have thought of that before charging out the door and leaving her alone.

Noah swung her around and hurried her out the front door and onto the porch. They both heard the sound of a motorcycle in the distance.

Fear had lent a feverish cast to her eyes, but Sydney was firmly in control. Which was more than Noah could say for himself. The knowledge that he'd left her to face a hidden danger gnawed at him, destroying his rationale. All he wanted was to get her someplace safe.

He took a deep breath. "We'll go for the car. No matter what happens, you keep going until you're inside with the doors locked."

"Okay."

Despite being scared to death, Sydney had guts. And even more startling, she still trusted him.

"Stay behind me," he said quickly. "I want you so close we're practically welded together."

She tried for a shaky smile. "Sounds kinky."

She was incredible. "Remind me later and I'll teach you something really kinky."

"I'll settle for the knowledge that you're wearing a bulletproof shirt."

"Nope. But it's my lucky shirt. I'm not dead yet."

"Noah, look!"

A Fools Point police car turned the corner, lights flashing.

"We won't have to put your shirt to the test after all," Sydney stated in obvious relief. "The cavalry is here."

"No faith in my lucky shirt, huh? One of the neighbors either heard the shots or saw two grown men running through the yards in ninety-nine-degree temperatures and came to the correct assumption," he agreed.

"Thank God."

He cupped her face, pushing the hair from her cheek, and kissed her quickly. Then he went down the steps to meet the policeman.

Officer Derek Jackstone listened while Noah explained what had happened, then Jackstone spoke into his radio, giving terse instructions. In short order, the Fools Point police force and several Montgomery County police officers descended on their doorstep.

Jackstone assigned one man to go through the house while he sent two others to scour the neighborhood. He stayed with Noah and Sydney.

"You're bleeding," Sydney said abruptly. She reached a finger to his cheek and it came away crimson.

"Just a scratch. I rolled down the embankment and almost ended up in the creek.'' And if one of his men had performed so poorly, the man would be looking for another line of work. ''When he started shooting I had to drop to avoid being hit and he got away.''

''Can you give me a description?'' Officer Jackstone asked.

''Six feet, dark hair, jeans and a T-shirt.''

''That sounds like the one I saw,'' Sydney agreed.

The policeman snorted. ''That's practically a summer uniform,'' he said in disgust. ''Color of the shirt?''

''White,'' they said in unison.

''Derek?'' a young officer shouted from the front porch. ''The house is clean but we've got a locked door upstairs.''

Officer Jackstone looked at Noah.

''Probably the attic,'' Noah told him.

''Do you have a key, Major?''

Noah shook his head. ''But you've got my permission to break it down.''

Jackstone nodded. Two more cars pulled up. ''Chief's here,'' Jackstone called to the other officer. ''Hold on and I'll back you up.''

Agent Wickowski approached with Chief John Hepplewhite. ''Mrs. Inglewood. Major,'' Chief Hepplewhite acknowledged. He ran blunt fingers through a shock of white hair that added years to his actual age.

''What happened this time?'' Wickowski demanded of Noah.

Noah recounted the events as tersely as possible. As a trained runner, he should have caught the first man easily. Explaining that he hadn't was embarrassing.

Officer Jackstone reappeared at the top of the steps. ''All clear, Chief.''

Wickowski immediately turned to Noah. ''Let's go inside and get out of this heat. We'd like a word with you in private, Major. Officer Jackstone will stay with you, Mrs. Inglewood.''

Reluctantly, Noah went into the den with the two men and covered the events once again, answering questions quickly, anxious to get back to Sydney.

"So the man you were chasing could have been this Alex Coughlin?'' Wickowski asked.

"Or Barry Fairvale, or Officer Jackstone or anyone else fitting that general description. I told you, I never got a clear look at his face.''

"But you did hear a motorcycle,'' Wickowski pressed.

"Heard it, but never saw it. How many motorcycles do you figure there are in and around this area?''

"Too many,'' Wickowski agreed. "But it's one more lead to follow.''

Frowning, Hepplewhite rubbed his chin. "I'll run a check on Fairvale and Coughlin.''

"Do that.'' Noah strode for the door, finished with the interview whether they were or not. They hadn't asked a thing they couldn't have asked in front of Sydney.

And the living room couch was empty. Jackstone stood guard on the staircase landing.

"Mrs. Inglewood is in the bathroom,'' he explained, starting down the steps as Noah went up.

"Chief?'' A voice called from the front porch. "We found shell casings.''

"Be right there.''

When Noah reached the second floor he found the bathroom door standing wide open, the room empty. Fear clutched at him until he heard someone moving in the bedroom next door.

The smell of fresh paint lingered in the humid air. He found Sydney standing beside a scarred maple dresser.

"Noah?" Excitement lanced in her voice. "Was this Jerome's room?"

"Yeah. It was."

Her perception surprised him. There was nothing personal to mark the room as his brother's former territory that he could see, but Noah briefly noted the bare mattress on the matching bed. The cover had been torn—or more likely, slit open with a knife.

"Then it looks like he owned a tape recorder after all."

A cold prickle walked up his back. As soon as he came abreast of her, Noah saw what she had seen. A wastebasket sat beside the tall dresser. Inside was a discarded plastic shopping bag bearing a local store logo. The open bag held a box and some packing paper, carelessly stuffed back inside. The contents were clearly labeled.

Noah removed the bag. "One of those small microcassette recorders," he said.

"But what did Jerome tape?"

Noah wondered the same thing. He delved into the bag for the receipt. Fishing it out, he studied the printed information.

"He bought it at the appliance store here in Fools Point two weeks ago. The credit card slip indicates he bought batteries and several tapes to go with the recorder. There's a wrapper for the batteries and for one of the tapes at the bottom of the bag."

"At least now we know what sort of tape to look for," she said softly.

"Yeah."

She pulled her hair back from her face to tuck it behind her ear, but worry lined her features. "We'd better have a look around."

"It's worth a try, but someone has already searched most of the house. I noticed the signs when we were going through the downstairs earlier.'' He indicated the torn mattress and her eyes widened.

''Is that what we interrupted when we came in?''

''Looks that way. I'd better get Hepplewhite and Wickowski. They need to figure out the who and why.''

Wickowski was excited by their discovery. Sydney sat beside Noah on the sofa, her hand in his. He wasn't sure which of them had reached for the other and he didn't care. The physical contact was somehow reassuring.

The police search yielded nothing beyond confirmation that someone had already searched the place pretty thoroughly. There were no tapes of any kind in the house. They lifted a few prints, but because there'd been tenants and work crews in here, most of them would be of little value unless they happened to hit pay dirt with a known felon.

Chief Hepplewhite arranged for a locksmith to come out right away and change all the locks on the house. By the time things were winding down, Noah felt as tired as Sydney looked.

''I'm too dirty to go anywhere like this. Let me grab my kit and some clean clothes and I'll take a quick shower while the police are still here. Then what do you say we go over to the restaurant and grab a bite to eat before we try one of the local motels?'' Noah asked.

''Whatever you want to do.''

''Are you okay?''

Sydney dipped her head, her hair falling forward to obscure her face. ''Sure. Why wouldn't I be?''

''You aren't a very good liar, Syd.''

''I'm just tired. Go get your shower. I'm fine, Noah.''

She was more than fine, but he was trying hard not to think about that. Noah showered in record time, finding towels in the linen closet as always. He returned to the living room feeling rejuvenated, only to discover Sydney half-asleep on the couch. Officer Jackstone and another officer were talking quietly in the hall foyer.

"Mrs. Inglewood looks beat," Jackstone offered. "You two planning to spend the night here?"

"Originally, but after today I'm not sure she's going to want to do that."

"Yeah. Here's the mail her friend was bringing to the house last night. We'll be keeping a close eye on this place tonight, so if you do stay here, just holler if you need anything at all."

"No phone," he reminded them. "I think we'll go out to the Bide Awhile Motel and—"

Jackstone shook his head. "Place burned down last month. The nearest motel is up in Frederick or down in Germantown."

"That's right. I noticed the motel was closed when I drove into town, but I forgot. Thanks. And thanks for responding so quickly this afternoon."

"No problem, Major. We generally respond real quick to a call about shots being fired in this neighborhood. The mayor lives on the court." He smiled. "Take it easy. Good night, Mrs. Inglewood."

Sydney had joined them silently. Now she added her thanks and watched them leave.

"Is it my turn for a shower?"

"Do you want one?" he asked in surprise.

She smiled. "What I really want is a long hot soak in a sauna, but I'll settle for a cup of herbal tea and a nap, not necessarily in that order."

"Can't help you with the sauna, but we can go get that tea and some food. You'll feel better after you eat. Then we'll drive down to Germantown and check into a motel so you can have an early night. Who knows, maybe we can find one with a sauna.''

He led her outside, pausing to collect the pile of mail that was sitting on the hall table.

"Don't you want to come back to the house tonight?"

''I thought you might prefer another anonymous motel.''

"It's a nice old house, Noah," she temporized.

"Yeah. It is." He'd been surprised by all the good memories that had come flooding back this afternoon while they'd been sitting there waiting.

"Fools Point was a good town to grow up in," he added.

"I can see that. I like your police chief and his men."

"Hepplewhite? He's not a native, but yeah, I like him too. He and his men ask smart questions. Wickowski seems to approve as well."

"I've been thinking about all this, Noah. There were only two men inside the bank that day. At least I never saw a third man. And today, there were only two men that we know of hiding inside the house."

"You think that lets Yosten and his crew out as suspects?"

She grew thoughtful. "Not necessarily, but those men *were* inside the house most of yesterday. I mean, the bathroom and bedroom had both been painted so they had plenty of time to look around. If they were involved, I don't see why they'd risk getting caught by coming back today. Maybe we were prejudiced by the way they looked. Lots of people wear jeans and T-shirts. And look how many men have dark hair. You do yourself."

Noah nodded. "Good point." He parked the car in the restaurant lot and came around to let her out. "On the other hand, maybe they returned to finish their search."

The bar area had a good capacity crowd already and the restaurant was doing a brisk business as well. He glimpsed the man calling himself Jake Collins, tending bar. Another man with dark hair, he realized.

The wait wasn't long. The food and the service were every bit as good as they'd been the night before. Noah recognized several people who were seated around them. A few even nodded in recognition, but no one approached their table.

Sydney ate with single-minded determination. Noah knew her thoughts weren't on the food at all, but the silence between them was relaxed rather than strained. She was a comfortable woman to be with, Noah realized. And every bit as brave as the men under his command. Of course, she didn't follow orders worth a damn. That thought made him smile. He had a feeling she'd be good at giving them.

"What's so funny?" she asked.

"I was thinking you'd make a good officer."

"Oh? Is that your polite way of telling me I tend to be bossy? Never mind, don't answer that, Major. I'm going to use the little officers' room for women. If you'll excuse me?"

He stood and followed her progress through the bar to where the bathrooms were. When he sat back down it came as no surprise that Jake Collins appeared at his table.

"Good evening, Major. Is everything satisfactory?" Collins asked smoothly.

Even the greeting didn't surprise Noah. In a small town like this one, everyone knew everyone else's business five minutes after they did. "Perfectly. Nice place."

The man took his measure and inclined his head. "Thank you. I heard you had some trouble this afternoon."

"A couple of prowlers broke into my dad's house."
Which wasn't technically true. The house was now his
and the police had discovered an unlocked basement window—no sign of a forced entry.

"Too bad. There isn't a lot of crime here in Fools
Point," Collins said neutrally.

"No, there never has been."

"I'm glad no one was hurt today."

Noah came to attention, trying to read behind the im-
placable mask of Jake Collins's face. Were his words intended as a threat, a warning or just a general comment?
Before Noah could decide, Sydney returned to the table.

"Mrs. Inglewood," Collins said in greeting. "Enjoy
your evening." He inclined his head again to include Sydney.

"Thank you," she said, stopping him when he would
have turned away. "I know I told you this before, but this
is a wonderful restaurant, Mr. Collins."

Collins hesitated. He looked oddly pleased by the sin-
cerity of her praise. "Thank you. Enjoy your visit in Fools
Point."

She sat down, watching him walk away before she
turned to Noah. "What was that all about?"

"Mr. Collins stops to chat with all his guests."

"I know. I meant between the two of you. I got the
feeling I was interrupting something."

"Not really. He just said something that started me
wondering."

"About what?"

"How much capital must be involved in opening a
place like this one."

"A lot, I'd imagine."

"Yeah."

Sydney looked across the room to where Jake Collins

had paused to talk with a table of six. "He has such empty eyes."

"What?"

Sydney shrugged. "He only lets you see the surface. He's an interesting-looking man, but I wouldn't want to have to be the woman to try and get beneath his exterior."

"I wouldn't like that much either."

For a moment, she simply stared at him. Noah was a little embarrassed by his hasty words, but he realized he meant them. He didn't like her finding Jake Collins "interesting."

"Didn't you say the town thinks he's part of the Mafia?"

"That's one of the rumors."

"I think I can see how it got started." When she smiled, he found himself smiling back. "At least we know he wasn't the man you chased from the house today."

"We do?"

Sydney arched her eyebrows. "Can you see the fastidiously dressed Jake Collins wearing a pair of jeans? Or smelling of garlic?" she added as an afterthought.

"Now that you mention it, no to both." His smile turned into a chuckle. "You never cease to amaze me, you know that?"

"Thank you. Noah, since we changed the locks at the house and we have both the police and the FBI keeping watch, do you want to waste money on another hotel or go back to the house tonight?"

"Wouldn't you be more comfortable in a hotel room?"

"Until these creeps are caught, I'm not going to be comfortable no matter where we spend the night."

He liked her choice of pronoun, but he didn't want to remind her that she'd been comfortable enough in his arms last night. The problem was, he was pretty sure he couldn't hold her again all night and promise to stay on top of the sheets this time. He'd become too aware of her as a woman. A woman he liked on every level.

The draw between them was getting harder and harder to ignore.

"You do know Wickowski thinks we're having an affair," she said calmly.

Noah nearly choked on his coffee. "What did you say?"

Complacently, she took another sip of her herbal tea. The small bruises at her neck were already changing colors, some fading to yellow-green while others were a dark reminder of the past few days.

"Maybe we should spend the night at the house," Sydney continued in a slow, thoughtful voice, "and hope the two creeps make another try. With the FBI and the local police watching they're bound to be caught."

"Sydney, new locks won't keep a determined person out of the house. Neither will police or FBI guardians."

"I know, but I have you to protect me."

Her faith astonished him. She'd come so close to danger this afternoon when he'd unintentionally put her at risk that he didn't know what to say.

"By staying at the house, maybe we can draw them out."

Noah flattened his hands on the tabletop hard enough to rattle the silverware. "You are *not* putting yourself at risk."

"Of course not. I'm not stupid."

"No. You aren't." He covered her hand with his. Instantly, the air became charged between them.

Sydney licked her lips. The gesture wasn't meant to be provocative, but there was no telling that to Noah's leaping imagination.

"How do you do that?" she asked softly.

"Do what?" He struggled to resist the impulse to stroke the back of her soft hand.

"Make me so aware of you with a simple touch."

Her frankness surprised him yet again, but he replied in kind. "In case you haven't noticed, you're having the same effect on me."

"Oh, I noticed. But I'm not going to go to bed with you, Noah."

His lips curved. "You already did."

The shared memory hung between.

"You know what I mean," she said finally.

He knew, but as a blush crept up her face, his body grew hard, wanting her.

His pulses leaped at the banked hunger in her eyes. She was no more immune to him than he was to her.

"What if I decide what I want is you?" he asked softly.

"Then you'll learn we don't always get what we want."

He leaned back, suddenly amused. "So cool. So confident. And you said *I* was intimidating."

A flicker of uncertainty. A trace of desire. Sydney wasn't as sure of herself as she'd like him to believe. And they were sharing the thought if not the action.

"I would love to take you to bed, Sydney. To watch that cool facade shatter like ice. To watch you melt and steam all around me in an explosion of need."

A curl of flame licked her eyes, warming the color already darkening her cheeks. Her eyelids lowered, thick lashes sweeping down to conceal the desire that made her fingers tremble beneath his hand.

"But you won't."

"No. I won't." And then, because he couldn't resist, he added, "Your virtue is as safe as you want it to be."

She surprised him by leaning back in her seat with a contemplative expression. "The problem is, what if I really don't want it to be safe?"

Her words drop-kicked his solar plexus. His mouth fell open and he had to remind himself to close it. She wasn't trying to be provocative. He could see she was actually thinking this over. He told his racing heart to stand down, but it wasn't listening.

She gave a ragged smile. With a toss of her head, the smile widened. "Don't worry, hero. Your virtue is safe, too. I've found sex is a highly overrated commodity."

"Maybe you've just had the wrong partners."

A honeyed warmth seemed to enter her expression. "Maybe I have."

And before he could think of a comeback for that, she rose and started for the door. Aware of more than one eye on them, Noah stood so fast he nearly overturned the chair. This playful side to her had taken him completely off guard.

As he followed the seductive sway of her hips, a chuckle built in the back of his throat. He'd never met a more maddening woman in all his life.

Chapter Eight

"I decided against staying at the house," Noah told her. "There are too many ways in and out and until we get a telephone installed, it's too risky. I'm not inclined to take any more chances."

"All right, but could we stop at a drugstore so I can pick up a few things?"

"No problem."

Big problem. His mind had been toying with the thought of taking Sydney to bed for so long that he was having to exert more control than normal. While he wrestled with his conscience, Sydney couldn't even seem to get out of the car without brushing up against him.

Her hand grazed his as she put items into the small basket he offered to carry for her. And his pulse rate picked up when he saw the racy cover on the paperback she selected. He was determined to do the right thing here, but the bath beads that the clerk rang up were nearly the final straw. The image of her soaking in a tub full of water was enough to make him sweat all the way to the motel he'd selected. How the devil was he going to share a room with Sydney again tonight without succumbing to the need pounding through his bloodstream?

"You know you're ruining my reputation completely,

don't you?'' she asked as they left the check-in counter and headed for the single room with two double beds he'd just rented.

Noah faltered. ''Does that worry you?''

''My reputation only worries me as it pertains to being a good jeweler. Anything else is my personal business.''

He looked at her to see if she was deliberately being provocative, but he caught her glancing at her bandaged hand.

''Your hand will heal, you know,'' he told her firmly.

''I'd like that guarantee in writing—right after I see your medical degree.''

He set the suitcases down to unlock the door and touched her shoulder in an offer of silent comfort. She leaned her cheek against his hand. ''Thank you.''

''For what?''

''For caring.''

He beat back the temptation to kiss her right there in full view of the parking lot and quickly opened the door. They stared at the small room in silence.

Two double beds on the second floor as ordered, but the room with its miniature kitchen at one end, complete with a two-burner stove, microwave and small refrigerator, gave new meaning to the word intimate.

''Cozy,'' she said neutrally.

''We had more space when we were sharing a single room with a king-size bed.''

''True, but look on the bright side, you can make me coffee in the morning.''

''I could if we'd bought any coffee,'' he agreed, thinking they should have gone back to his father's nice big house with its great big bedrooms with doors that shut and even locked from the inside.

''Want to go back out and do some more shopping?''

"At the risk of missing an opportunity for breakfast in bed, I think I'll pass."

Noah smiled. "Probably a good decision on your part. I always figured they created restaurants because of the fire hazard associated with letting people like me near a kitchen."

"No good with gourmet dinners, huh?"

"Not unless they come covered in plastic with instructions like punch holes and rotate after three minutes. But you'll like this bathroom," Noah informed her after looking around. "It's nearly as big as the entire bedroom. No sauna, but the tub is clean and deep. It would probably even hold two," he added before he could stop himself.

Pink tinted her cheeks, but she reached inside the drugstore bag and waved a small package. "Only if they both want to smell like gardenias."

"Drat. I'm not sure, but I think that just might cost me my next promotion."

Sydney chuckled.

"But I could risk scrubbing your back for you," he offered with a teasing grin.

"Such a considerate person. I'll get back to you on that."

But her gaze looked the tiniest bit wistful as she looked inside the spacious room.

"Hey, seriously, if you want to take a bath, go ahead." Anything to delay the conversation he was going to have with her tonight.

Sydney hesitated. "It *would* feel good."

"Then do it. I'll get some ice for the sodas and see what's on television."

Sydney stared at the large tub and knew she was weakening. A nice soaking bath would feel wonderful after the stressful day. But she could no longer tell herself that

Noah wasn't interested in her *that way*. Nor could she pretend the desire was all one-sided. The currents between them practically vibrated in the visible range. Despite the fact there were at least a million reasons not to feel this way, she was the one lusting after Noah.

"Hey." He cupped her chin. "Earth to Sydney."

Sydney shivered. What was it about this man that drew her so? She barely resisted the impulse to draw his face down to hers and see if she could break down that rigid control he exhibited most of the time.

"Take your bath, Sydney." He stepped back, saving her from temptation. "I already got a shower, remember?"

As if she could forget. He smelled so darn good. And he'd even taken time to run a razor lightly over his chin, raising her crazy hopes that maybe he had more in mind than just sleeping tonight.

It was crazy. On the one hand she wanted him desperately. On the other, she kept telling herself making love with Noah would be a mistake. She wasn't into one-night stands. These were just her surging hormones kicking in or something. They were going to share a room, not each other.

But would it really be so awful if they did share more?

"I'll be right back," he told her. "The ice machine is just down the hall. Yell, and I can be here in a millisecond."

"I'm not worried. Go get your ice."

But she was worried. Noah exuded a masculinity that drew her like a magnet. He was also funny and kind. Too bad she'd met the wrong brother first.

Guilt was never far from her mind when she thought of Jerome. But it was the guilt of a survivor and was tempered by her strong suspicion that Jerome had taken some part in the very crime that had killed him.

What was on the tapes that the robbers wanted so badly? And where were those tapes now?

She filled the tub with hot steamy water and gardenia-scented oil. She was getting better at undressing one-handed, though the bra closure took some effort. And she had to be careful climbing into the tub one-handed. But the water felt wonderful and despite the difficulty of reading one-handed, the romance novel she'd purchased proved to be light and quirky.

Unfortunately, it also proved to be one of the author's steamier works. Reading about a hero and heroine in a room filled with erotica was probably not the best choice she could have made when she was so aware of Noah prowling around on the other side of that flimsy door.

Despite the book's fast pace, she kept finding her thoughts straying to Noah. Since she couldn't concentrate, she set the book on the floor and leaned back, closing her eyes. This was the first real peace she'd felt since waking in the middle of this living nightmare.

If only she'd heeded her earlier instincts and hadn't rushed into marriage with Jerome. He'd been so charmingly persuasive and life had seemed to be in a hurry to pass her by. She hadn't met a single man she wanted to live with, let alone marry. And sex for sex's sake wasn't worth the risk. Her two encounters had left her emotionally empty and unsatisfied.

Ironically, in the end she'd given in to Jerome's request primarily because he wasn't interested in sex. He'd offered friendship and respect instead—or so she'd thought. More importantly, he'd offered her a chance for the family they both wanted. The biggest irony of all was that she'd contemplated single parenthood and decided it was unfair to the child. Now here she was, a single parent anyhow. She could have skipped all those months of unhappiness with Jerome and just had the fertilization process done on her own. There must be a cosmic joke in there some- where.

Noah rapped on the door, startling her. "Everything okay?"

"Yes." The water had started to cool. "I'll be out in a few minutes."

"No hurry. I just wanted to be sure you didn't fall asleep and drown on me."

"Thanks a lot." She sat up and reached for the wash- cloth, wondering what he'd do if she asked him to come in and soap her back as he'd offered.

Why couldn't she stop thinking of Noah that way? In- stead of shocking her, the idea kindled all sorts of naughty images. She ran the cloth across her breasts, which had become extremely sensitive to the slightest touch. The nipples instantly beaded to tiny hard points.

"Okay guys, you're not helping here," she whispered.

As she lathered her legs, she wondered what it would be like to have Noah's hand running that cloth up and down instead.

"Not good, Sydney. You're letting this imagery carry you away."

"Did you say something?" Noah called out.

Sydney grimaced, embarrassed by her wayward thoughts. "Just talking to myself."

His voice dropped suggestively on the other side of the door. "Saying anything interesting?"

No doubt he'd think so. "Just wishing for a handser- vant," she told him.

The handle turned. She only had a moment to yank the

shower curtain closed before Noah opened the door. "What do you need?" he asked seriously.

"Nothing! I was kidding!"

"Oh. Sorry. I thought you were having a problem. Hey, you're getting your book all wet. Want me to move it?"

"Yes. Fine. Take it in the other room. I'll be out in a minute."

"Okay."

She held her breath, watching his outline against the curtain as he bent beside the tub and removed her book. Her heart pounded, but it wasn't fear she was feeling. It was anticipation.

Absurd. The moment she heard the door click shut, Sydney finished washing and released the drain. Only then did she discover the difficulty standing one-handed presented. The tub was slick with the fragrant oil and her muscles were a little too relaxed. For one horrible minute she thought she might have to call Noah back inside to help her out of the tub.

She managed to stand without falling, but she got the upper part of her cast wet in the process.

"Blast!"

"You okay in there?" Noah called.

"Perfect."

"Do you need some help getting out?"

"Not anymore."

She stepped onto the bathmat and toweled herself briskly as best she could. Despite the steam that coated the mirrors, the air conditioner was sending goose bumps up and down her body. She struggled into the slippery turquoise gown, noting that her breasts were not only more sensitive, but seemed larger. Was she gaining weight, or was this part of the pregnancy changes? She ran her hand over her belly, looking for signs that she was filling out there too. She needed to get those books on pregnancy that the doctor had recommended so she'd know what was normal and what wasn't.

For the first time, she accepted the wonder of this miracle. A new life was growing inside of her. A child to nurture and love. The heady sensation was incredibly exciting. Almost euphoric. She'd wanted this for so long. As she wiped uselessly at the mirror and combed her hair and brushed her teeth, she let the excitement fill her with pleasure. A girl or boy. She didn't care. Just please let the child be healthy.

Draping the bath towel around her shoulder in lieu of a robe, Sydney finally opened the bathroom door.

Noah lay propped on two pillows on the bed near the door, her romance novel firmly in hand. He looked up when she entered, maintaining his page. His gaze swept her with warm approval and an almost sensual heat. He'd unbuttoned his shirt and looked altogether too much like a romance hero for her peace of mind.

"Feel better?" he asked gently.

Her imagination was running away with her. There was nothing provocative in that question.

"Much."

She told herself to cross the short distance separating them and climb into the other bed, but her gaze remained fixed on Noah.

"Interesting book," he drawled.

She decided it was her highly charged mood that gave his smile a seductive quality. He wasn't coming on to her—even if his gaze was running over her like warm honey.

"I've never read one of these before."

She had to clear her throat. "Most men haven't."

"They ought to pick one up sometime. They don't know what they're missing."

Now that *had* been suggestive.

"I suppose you think they're nothing but women's erotica."

Noah raised his eyebrows at her defensive tone. "On the contrary. I like the way the author uses humor. The sensuality is threaded through the action quite nicely. Even though the plot is a bit of a stretch."

"It is, huh?"

"Sure. A man would never kidnap a woman like this."

His words surprised her, but they released her from her self-imposed reluctance to come closer. She walked between the two beds and sat down facing him. An open cola stood on the nightstand beside a glass filled with ice.

"How would he kidnap her?"

"He wouldn't. If he desired her the way the author suggests, he'd simply kiss her until she either slapped him silly or invited him into her bed."

He set the book down beside him, spine up to mark his page.

"I see. And does that generally work for you he-men types?"

Despite her best intention, something inside her responded to his slow, deadly smile. Once again his gaze ran over her body like a warm caress. Her nipples tightened in immediate response and a vibrating tingle began low in her belly.

"Nothing always works, but we he-men type tend to be pretty primitive. Surround us with erotic art—" his eyes flicked in amusement toward the watercolor reproduction of a seascape that hung over the bed. "And add an extremely sexy, desirable woman who smells like an exotic flower." He sat up and slowly swung his legs over the side of the bed, never taking his gaze from her. "How can a woman hold a man completely responsible for his behavior?"

Their knees were practically touching. His eyes locked with hers as heat licked her insides. Her nipples were almost painfully hard.

"So how *would* you behave?"

His open shirt drew her gaze to the exposed area of his chest. She gripped the comforter to keep from reaching out to explore that chest.

Noah stood abruptly. In front of her eyes was the proof of how dangerous this word game had become. Noah was not unmoved by the exchange. She fisted her hand more tightly on the comforter to keep it from bridging the distance between them. Would it be so wrong to give in to this consuming need she had to taste him, touch him... make love with him?

Noah came and sat down beside her without warning. The brush of his body against her froze her to the spot. She was afraid to move and afraid not to move.

"Sydney, we need to talk."

"I...thought that was what we were doing."

"No, I mean really talk. Are you cold?"

"N-no."

"You're shivering."

"The air conditioner is a little cool," she lied.

Noah smiled, seeing the lie for what it was. He rested his hand on her shoulder. "I could turn up the heat."

Her eyes smiled first and then her mouth. The slow smile of longing nearly melted his resolve.

"If it gets any hotter," he told her, "we're both going to sizzle."

"Sounds...promising."

A look of pure desire nearly loosened his control. "It does, doesn't it? But we have to talk."

"And that sounds serious."

Slowly, as if it were a vital piece of clothing and she were performing a sensual striptease for his benefit, she drew the damp towel from around her shoulders. Her expression said she knew exactly what she was doing. Her gaze dropped to his crotch where she couldn't fail to see what she was doing.

"Sydney?" He was fighting the strong urge to run his finger over the expanse of skin she'd just exposed to see if it felt as silken as it looked. The promise of that look was almost his undoing.

She lifted her chin and met his eyes. Determination, hesitation and a wild fierce desire all came together in her expression. His insides knotted in reaction.

"Are you trying to seduce me?"

"Yes, but I'm not doing it right, am I?" She bit at her lower lip nervously. "I'm a little new at this...so I could use some help here."

He wanted to chuckle. Sydney was always doing or saying the unexpected. "Trust me, you're doing just fine."

"But?"

"Does it look like I have any buts?"

"Well, actually, now that you mention it, I have noticed that you have a very nice butt, Major."

Noah did laugh then, but quickly shook his head. "Sydney..."

She sighed. "You aren't going to cooperate, are you?"

"It's just that we need to talk about the baby."

Her face lifted to his, startled. "Oh. Does my pregnancy turn you off? I'm sorry. I thought since I'm barely showing yet—it has made my breasts larger—more sensitive—but—''

He groaned and closed his eyes, whipping them open when she laid her hand on his arm. The sheer power of her touch left him defenseless. ''Sydney—''

''I know I'm not very experienced. I've never been very interested in sex so I'm probably going about this all wrong.''

Her fears would have been laughable if she hadn't been so insecure. Noah knew it was a mistake, but he couldn't stand the uncertainty on her face.

''C'mere.'' He pulled her forward, letting the tops of her breasts graze his arm. Her heart was beating much too fast. He could see the pulse point jumping in her neck. His own heart rate was none too steady either. He needed to terminate this erotic tease before it was too late.

''Are you going to kiss me again?'' she breathed against his jaw.

His hand reached for her hair before he could stop himself. He threaded his fingers through the soft fall and found himself unconsciously drawing her face up to his.

''We need to talk.''

''Please. Can't it wait?'' And she pulled his head down the rest of the way.

It was almost a relief when his lips lightly kissed hers. She'd very nearly lost her nerve completely. Now a spark of sheer lust licked through her, setting her blood on fire. Very gently, he parted his lips and sucked at the sensitive skin of her neck.

Like an extended bowstring, she arched in his arms. He moved on, alternating butterfly kisses with tender nips and tiny kisses against the highly sensitized skin.

Need became a flash flame of desire. She twisted to face him, nearly smacking him in the face with her cast

in her haste to capture his mouth. Their lips fused. All
thoughts of stopping fled.

Her hand sought his chest, playing lightly over the hair
as she ran her hand back and forth. She couldn't get
enough of his mouth. When his hand skimmed the tops
of her breasts, she arched to allow him better access. But
Noah suddenly stopped.

"Are you sure, Sydney? I need to know now if this is
what you want."

Sydney stared at him, quivering all over. How could he
question her need?

"I want. Please don't stop."

He made a noise low in his throat and drew her mouth
back to his. Her senses heightened as never before. Their
tongues tangled in a mating ritual she'd read about but
never experienced. Not like this.

Never like this.

When he stopped again, she moaned in protest until she
realized he was simply trying to lower the bodice of her
gown, to give himself access to more than just the tops
of her breasts. He drew a nipple inside the heat of his
mouth and her world spun wildly out of control.

The orgasm hit her with stunning force, shocking her
with the pleasure pain of fulfillment. His eyes glowed with
wild excitement as he watched her tumbling over the edge
of pleasure. She should be embarrassed. She *was* embarrassed. But Noah didn't give her a chance to pull away.

"You're beautiful, Sydney."

He kissed her, gently, more tenderly than anyone had
ever kissed her before. The overload of sensation brought
tears to her eyes and he kissed them away as well. Fisting
his hands in her hair, he kissed her over and over again,
finally running one hand down and across her body, sliding the fabric of her gown provocatively against her skin.

As incredible as it seemed, she realized that far from being over, the sensations were building all over again. Noah trailed his hand lower, slipping it beneath the fabric of her gown to stroke her inner thigh. His touch moved higher. Lightly, his hand skimmed across that hair, bringing ripples of delightful expectancy.

"Take off your shirt," she begged.

"I thought you'd never ask," he teased.

Noah slipped out his shirt, then tugged the straps of her gown down her arms, baring both her breasts. His eyes grew hot as he stared at her, driving her deeper and deeper into the maelstrom of wanting. With erotic deliberation, he lowered himself over her, rubbing his chest lightly against her exposed nipples.

Reaction, hot and instantaneous, stabbed her guts. She pulled him down, planting wild kisses along his collarbone, and wishing for two good hands to run across the planes of his chest. Instead her hand stroked the bulge behind his pants.

"Take off your pants. I can't do it with only one hand."

His eyes twinkled with humor. "I knew you were the type who liked to give orders."

He unsnapped his pants and lowered the zipper. The sound was erotically loud. She waited impatiently while he undressed. His size unnerved her, but he didn't give her time to worry. While she tentatively stroked him, Noah bent to kiss her inner thigh. Her breath caught as he alternated soft kisses, with openmouthed light sucking that left her writhing in desire.

His hand skimmed the apex of her thighs lightly, making her crave a more intimate touch. Noah smiled, one of those incredibly hot smiles. Slowly, he cupped her there and she gripped him tightly. While her breath trapped in her throat, he eased one finger inside of her.

"Noah!"

"Is it okay? Do you like me touching you like this?"

"Yes." The agreement was drawn from her on a gasp of pleasure as he inserted a second finger. The feeling was incredible.

"It's been a long time for you, hasn't it?"

"Yes." Longer than he knew. And it had never been anything like this.

He withdrew his hand and she would have cried out in protest, but his mouth fused with hers and he lowered himself over her. As he probed for entrance, she welcomed him greedily, clenching around him as he penetrated her. She was rewarded by a masculine groan of pleasure.

"Wrap your legs around me," he ordered.

She obeyed, and he slid more deeply inside. Her breasts rubbed against his wiry chest hair while her body filled with the scent and feel of him. They kissed deeply, letting the feverish rhythm take them to that incredible brink.

Noah stiffened. She found herself joining him in a new plunge over the edge of pleasure.

For long glorious minutes afterward, they lay there. She didn't want him to ever move, but eventually he eased away and rolled to one side. Only then did other sights and sounds penetrate her sensual haze. She became aware of the noisy air conditioner beside the other bed, and the chill air quickly cooled their sweat-slicked skin.

"Roll over a minute so I can pull the covers down," he said.

While it had been her intention to never move again, she did and was happy when he slid beneath the covers beside her. He tugged her body against the length of his and settled comfortably. She should probably be filled

with all sorts of recriminations, but all she felt was satisfied.

"If that's what you he-men do in a room filled with
erotic art," she said quietly, "I wonder how you'd handle
a room filled with erotic statuary."

Noah's chuckle became a full-throated laugh. The rich
sound soothed her almost as much as the hand that
snugged her closer still.

"You're something else, Sydney."

"Uh-huh." She yawned hugely. "I never knew it could
be like that."

His hand stroked her arm. "Me either."

The two words brought an even greater wash of contentment. Sydney closed her eyes. In seconds, she was
asleep.

Noah lay beside her and tried to sort through a mix of
emotions. This was going to complicate everything. He
hadn't meant to take her to bed. He'd only kept up the
sexual teasing to take the edge off her discomfort with
the situation when she first came out of the bathroom.

He should have known better—and maybe he had. He'd
wanted Sydney almost right from the start. He just hadn't
planned to take her.

His brother had a lot to answer for—not the least of
which was making Sydney doubt her femininity. Her un-
tutored responses had all but driven him out of his mind.

He wasn't sorry for what they'd just done, but he had
a feeling she would be, once she had time to think things
over. He would have to move quickly. He wondered how
long the waiting period was for a marriage license in the
state of Maryland. It didn't matter that he'd never wanted
any hostages to fortune. He had them now. Sydney and
her baby belonged to him.

His commanding officer was going to be surprised. And

probably none too pleased. He still had six months before his tour of duty was up. Thankfully, he'd be eligible for early retirement, and all that money he'd set aside and invested over the years was going to come in handy. He wondered if Sydney would be willing to live in Fools Point. And then he wondered what he was going to do with the rest of his life.

Funny. He'd never thought about life outside of the Rangers. In fact, he hadn't held a civilian job since he was seventeen. He hoped he could adapt. He'd have to. There was no way he was going to try and have a family and a military career. He'd heard enough officers' wives complain. It was simply too hard on the family.

With a yawn, he reached for the light switch, trying not to disturb Sydney. When she shifted he paused to study her sleeping features. He'd told her she was beautiful— and she was. But even more important, he'd grown to like the woman behind those features. He'd find a way to adapt to civilian life.

Noah woke to find the right side of his body numb again because her soft weight was curled firmly against him. It took effort not to kiss that sweet mouth into wakefulness. Instead, he slipped carefully out of bed, snatched up his shaving kit, and padded into the bathroom. The feathery scent of gardenias not only hung in the air, but clung to his skin. He almost hated to wash the fragrance away.

He took his time shaving and showering, prolonging the anticipation of seeing her again. He hoped she wouldn't regret what had happened, but either way, they needed to talk and plan.

She was perched on one of the bar stools when he reentered the room, the forgotten mail strewn in front of her.

Her expression immediately made him forget any plans to talk.

"Noah! Look!" She waved a yellow slip of paper, her eyes dancing with excitement.

"What's that?"

"It was on top in this pile of mail you brought inside."

"I picked up the mail at the house."

"I remember, but Noah, this is addressed to me."

"Chief Hepplewhite gave me the stuff Laura was bringing you from the apartment."

"I know," she said excitedly, "but this is addressed to me at the house in Fools Point!"

Noah took the paper from her fingers. The mailman had tried to deliver a parcel to the house that had been sent by registered mail. Since it required a signature, the mailman had delivered a yellow reminder to come by the post office to claim the item.

"Only one person would have sent something to me at an address I didn't even know existed. Jerome must have mailed the tapes to me to throw off suspicion, Noah. What else can it be? I've got no connection to that house. And that would explain why those men want me. There must be something on the tapes that will incriminate them, probably even identify them."

Her enthusiasm was contagious. It really was the only thing that made any sense.

"We'll finally know what's on those tapes that's so valuable. If you're finished in the bathroom, I'm going to get ready. We can drive to the post office and collect the package. Once we turn it over to the FBI, those men will be too busy running away to bother with me."

He hoped she was right. This was the first time he'd seen a sparkle in her eyes. Foolishly, part of him wished that he had been the one to put it there, but the sane part of him was simply glad that this was coming to an end.

She stood and offered her mouth for a kiss.

The simple trust of that action unbalanced him completely. "No regrets?"

Her eyes were wide, completely guileless. He saw nothing but confidence and acceptance in her expression.

"Should I have?"

"No, Sydney. None at all."

"Good—" she kissed him quickly "—'cause I don't have any." And she hurried into the bathroom fairly bubbling with excitement.

Noah smiled after her, a bit ruefully. Would he ever understand her mind?

She'd donned another pair of shorts and pink print top. And while there was nothing overtly sexy about the top, the shorts were very short shorts leaving a wonderful expanse of leg for him to watch. She seemed so unaware of her sensuality. It delighted and amazed him.

"All set?"

"Yes. Thank heavens for front-clasp bras."

He had a sudden strong urge to unbutton that blouse and check out the front-clasp bra for himself. "I could have helped."

"I don't think so," she scolded. "We'd never leave this motel room."

"Would that be so bad?"

Her expression softened in memory. "No." She gazed around. "I'm always going to have fond memories of this place."

"Me too. Want to take your clothes off and get naked again?" He raised his eyebrows suggestively just to hear her laugh again.

Sydney obliged and slapped him playfully. "Later, mister. First we turn this evidence over to the police."

That brought all humor to a halt. "We should call Wickowski."

"At seven twenty-five in the morning? I know he's dedicated, Noah, but even the FBI must sleep sometime. Would he be in his office this early? Why don't we wait and see what the package contains first."

"I'll call and leave a message," he temporized. She was only a little smug when she turned out to be right. Wickowski wasn't in yet. He left the message and they gathered their belongings and repacked the car.

"This is going to be the most traveled African violet plant I've ever owned," she told him. "I only hope I don't kill it by moving it around so much."

"If you do, I'll buy you another one to replace it."

She smiled. "How did you know they were my favorites?"

"I'd love to take psychic credit here, but the truth is, I didn't. You already had two large bouquets of cut flowers, so when I saw something different, I bought it."

"I'm glad. Someday I'm going to have a garden and a greenhouse filled with plants."

"A real homebody, huh?"

She peered at him from beneath lowered lashes. "While other women dreamed of exotic careers, my dream was always to have a big old house filled with kids and animals and plants to love. Not very modern of me, I'm afraid."

Noah relaxed, envisioning the scene. Until now, he hadn't given much thought to the baby as a real live human being, but he could picture Sydney inside his father's old house, surrounded by dogs and cats and plants and kids. Two or three at least.

"Hey, where'd you go?" she asked. "Am I boring you?"

"Not at all. I like your dream. I just didn't hear a husband mentioned in that scenario."

She blushed and shifted uncomfortably. Noah decided to let her off the hook when she changed the subject.

"The tapes mean Jerome was helping the bank robbers, don't they?" she asked.

"You knew that was a possibility, Syd. I suspect we're going to find Jerome was deep in debt. He always liked to live well."

"Yes. I never thought about where the money came from, but now…" She shrugged. "I wouldn't have gone back to him, you know. No matter how much money he had. Our problems weren't about money."

"I know."

"I never thought of myself as a quitter, Noah, but I began to realize our marriage was a terrible sham that was never going to work no matter what I did. We couldn't communicate. Not on any level. I couldn't believe how fast or how much he changed as soon as the artificial insemination was over. It was as if all he wanted from me was the child."

Guilt slammed him. He should have spoken up this morning instead of building a marriage of sand castles in his mind. Sydney might very well view his proposal the same way.

"What did you expect from marriage?" he asked cautiously.

"I thought we'd work together to build a bond based on trust and sharing and mutual goals," she explained. "But he changed so quickly from the man I thought I knew into this demanding, impossible person I didn't even want to know."

Noah saw she wasn't trying to score any points off his own tendency to dominate. In fact, she sounded puzzled and uncertain.

"You're a pretty strong personality, too, Sydney. I'd think you could hold your own against any orders he might try to give."

"Maybe. If things had been normal. But Jerome wouldn't listen. He made arbitrary decisions and expected me to blindly obey. When I refused, he went into rages."

Noah gripped the steering wheel more tightly. "He hit you?"

"No. But I suspect it would have come to that soon enough. His anger seemed to be escalating. His temper was unpredictable. Looking back, I think you were right that he was using our marriage to move up in the world of banking. He was promoted to assistant manager right after we announced our engagement and he was up for another promotion right before he was killed."

"I'm sorry."

Sydney shook her head. "It was my own fault. The whole thing taught me a valuable lesson. I'll never be tempted to rush into something as important as a marriage ever again."

Noah nearly ran the car off the road.

"Noah! Look out!"

"Sorry. What do you mean by that? Are you saying you don't ever plan to get married again?" His stomach knotted even tighter as he saw all his carefully laid plans mentally collapsing in ruin about his head.

"Believe me, marriage isn't something I plan to jump into again anytime soon, if ever. Isn't that our turnoff coming up?"

"What? Yes." He switched lanes, making mental switches as well. He'd had his game plan perfectly orchestrated in his mind, only to discover his opponent had left and he was playing solitaire on an empty field.

"Noah, are you okay?"

"Sorry, I was thinking about what you said."

She'd married Jerome a few months after meeting him. If she thought that had been too soon, it was highly unlikely she was going to accept a proposal from Noah after days rather than months. Time to retreat and regroup. Obviously, she considered what happened between them last night nothing more than mind-blowing sex.

Noah pulled into the parking lot behind the post office and blinked in surprise.

The small brick building was surrounded by police.

Chapter Nine

Police Chief John Hepplewhite looked from the yellow slip of paper to each of them in turn. "You should have reported this right away," he said mildly.

"This *is* right away," Noah explained. "We found it early this morning." He surveyed the damage inside the post office and shook his head. "Apparently our intruders found it yesterday."

"But why didn't they take it with them?" Sydney asked.

"They must not have recognized the importance until later on," Noah said reasonably.

Hepplewhite walked over to the usually unflappable postmistress, Bianca Tooley. Her seasoned face creased with more animation than Noah could ever remember seeing on it. A fixture at the post office ever since Noah could remember, she always had a black Labrador named Spider at her side. Her current retriever sat watching the commotion from sad, jaded eyes.

Miss Tooley, who didn't hold with any of that "Miz" nonsense, was giving the chief one of her cold-eyed stares. She looked pointedly at him and said something short and probably pithy, knowing Miss Tooley.

"We'll look for the package," Hepplewhite said a few

minutes later, "but I think we can assume it's what the thieves were after. If so, it isn't likely we're going to find it. Are you going to be around?"

"Actually, we need to go back into D.C. and check Sydney's apartment." At his side, she tensed, but didn't protest. "I've also got to make arrangements for Jerome's car and run a few errands, but we'll be happy to check back."

"Fair enough."

Nothing had prepared them for the devastation they found inside Jerome's apartment. Where the burglars had ransacked Laura's, they'd destroyed this one. Everything breakable was smashed beyond recognition. Sofas and chairs had been slashed open, reminding Noah of the mattress back at his place.

"Someone was angry. This looks like spite to me."

"How could they do all this damage, yet no one heard a thing?" Sydney whispered, stricken by the extent of the mess.

He touched her back in silent support. "Most people work, Syd. If I was a burglar, I'd go in during the day posing as a repair person. No one would look twice."

"So where do we start? I'm not even sure what we're looking for. If Jerome had any tapes here they would have found them. I mean, look at this mess, Noah."

"I know. I need to find his insurance information and his bank records and everything else we'll need to close out his estate."

Sydney shuddered. "Try his bedroom. He kept all his files in there. I'm going to check my plants." She picked her way carefully through the rubble.

Pushing aside a bent piece of modern art, Noah knew instinctively that the expensive furnishings had belonged to Jerome, not Sydney. A woman who could enthuse over wainscoting and an old house wouldn't select a black leather sectional couch for her living room. Nor did he see Sydney watching enough television to account for the wide screen set that lay smashed all over the carpeting.

He heard a soft moan and quickly ran for the back bedroom. Sydney stood just inside, staring at the ruin. A multitude of plants had been dumped, kicked and otherwise sadly mutilated. Their dirt had been strewn over the contents of a very feminine bedroom.

Sydney stooped over a white African violet that appeared to be still intact even though its powder-blue pot was shattered.

"Want me to find something to put it in?" he offered gently.

"Please."

She kept her back to him, but her voice was sad. He touched her back lightly before going to the kitchen to see what he could find. She accepted the unbroken glass bowl with a soft thank you. Noah watched her scoop dirt from the floor, carefully avoiding the shards of pottery, to coat the bottom of the bowl. She placed the plant tenderly inside, adding more dirt with equal care.

"Want some help saving the rest?"

"No. Thank you. There isn't much left to save. I'll do what I can. You start going through Jerome's stuff so we can get out of here."

He hesitated, then did as she asked. He found Jerome's checkbook right away, and several bills. The total staggered him, despite what he'd half expected. Clothing was the biggest expenditure, but a number of meals and other items had been charged as well. It took time before he realized there were no insurance papers inside the room. "Sydney?"

"What is it?" She came to the doorway pulling a large suitcase on wheels behind her.

Noah eyed the suitcase.

"I packed my clothing. I don't want to have to come back."

He nodded in understanding. "Is there any particular place where Jerome kept his personal papers?"

"He had a small strongbox."

"I found the box. The lock was broken and it's empty."

"They probably dumped the contents."

Noah shook his head. "I found his checkbook and a collection of bills. My brother really did have a thing for expensive clothing, didn't he?"

"He dressed well, yes. So he was in debt?"

"More than I figured, but I can't find any insurance papers, no tax forms, none of the sort of papers we're going to need to close down his estate."

"What would bank robbers want with those?"

"I don't know. Can you think of anyplace else he would have kept them?"

She started to shake her head and paused, brushing the hair from her eyes. "You know, right before I left, he asked me to sign as a co-owner on a safety deposit box. Maybe he moved them all to the bank."

"Did he give you a key?"

"No, but as his wife, that shouldn't be a problem, should it?"

"I don't think so, but I don't know anything about safety deposit boxes. If your name is on the signature card—"

"It is."

"Then I'm sure we can get in somehow. Let me take another quick look around and see if I can find his key."

The search proved fruitless. Noah gazed about the room. "Did Jerome ever take you to a place called Arnie's?"

Sydney looked up from the pile of clothing she was stacking on the bed. "No. I've never heard of it, why?"

"Jerome ran up quite a tab there in the last month or so."

She shrugged. "He wasn't much for cooking."

Noah continued to frown. "Have you seen a phone book anywhere in all this mess?"

"It should be out in the kitchen near the telephone. Why?"

"I thought maybe we'd take a ride over to Arnie's. If Jerome was a regular there, maybe someone can tell us something about who he's been talking to the past couple of months."

Sydney brightened, obviously happy for any excuse to leave.

Arnie's turned out to be a bar or club sort of place in a neighborhood that wasn't particularly good. Sydney noticed Noah frowning as soon as they turned down the street.

"This is a bad idea," he announced.

"It'll be fine. It's broad daylight, Noah. While I wouldn't walk around at night, we shouldn't have any problems at this hour. Look at all the traffic going by."

"Yeah." But he was eyeing a young woman in skin-tight shorts with a minuscule bandeau top, wearing uncomfortably high heels. She slouched against an orange brick wall near the corner. With bright red nails you could see at a distance, she pushed at a tangle of red hair that clashed with the wall and her nails.

Noah's jaw set in a familiar line.

"There's a lot right over there," Sydney quickly pointed out.

The attendant was willing to let them park—for an astronomical fee. And he eyed Noah with unabashed approval. Noah put an arm around her waist as they started walking. "Stay right beside me."

"Am I supposed to protect you from the prostitutes or the lot attendant?"

He flashed her an amused look. "Both. You never fail to amaze me, you know that?"

"Hey, I'm a city girl, Noah."

He squeezed her waist lightly. "Then you know this is a lousy idea. I don't want anyone mistaking what *you're* doing down here."

"Oh! I hadn't thought of that." She giggled and he tipped his head.

"What's so funny?"

"The idea of someone mistaking me for a street walker."

"There's nothing funny about that."

His look was fiercely protective. She was both flattered and a little annoyed that he thought she couldn't take care of herself. But then, she thought drolly, he hadn't seen many signs of the latter.

Noah halted in front of the heavy inlaid door marked Arnie's. Thick, colored-glass windows prevented them from seeing inside the place.

"Maybe we should just give this information to the police and let them come ask the questions."

"Chicken." Sydney opened the door before Noah could stop her.

It took her eyes several minutes to adapt to the air-conditioned darkness after the bright humid heat outside.

A figure at the far end of the bar rose and scurried away, but every other head in the place turned to stare at them.

Undaunted, Sydney strode forward. The bar ran almost the length of the place, culminating in a tiny stage. In front of that was a small area cleared for dancing, and beyond were tables and even a few intimate booths. Despite the darkness, the interior looked clean.

There weren't a whole lot of people inside and all of them male, Sydney noticed, suddenly much too aware of her own skimpy outfit. While it wasn't like the woman's on the street corner, Sydney still wished she'd worn slacks. But most of the stares moved quickly from her to Noah. Hardly surprising considering how intimidating he looked.

She drew him forward, despite the resistance she sensed and selected the table closest to the door. Reluctantly, Noah pulled out a chair and sat beside her. A waiter approached, looking bemused. "Help you?" he asked.

"Yes, I'll have an iced tea," Sydney announced.

People continued staring at them. Despite the piped-in music and the noise from the television over the bar, it was awfully silent inside the restaurant.

"I'll have a beer," Noah said softly, in a voice that brooked no argument. "Anything on draft."

The waiter hesitated. "Okay," he agreed and turned away.

Sydney leaned next to Noah. She didn't have to lean too far. He'd moved his chair so close she was practically in his lap.

"Noah, I think this is a gay bar."

There was a tic in his jaw. "You noticed."

"You knew?"

"Not until it was too late." He slid his arm around her shoulders.

"Should we leave?"

"No. They figure we're tourists who don't know any better. Just keep your eyes on me and look fascinated."

"Fascinated?"

He lifted her hand and deliberately began to stroke it. "Can you manage enthralled?"

When he touched her like that, she could barely manage a coherent thought.

"Perfect. You're doing fine."

"So are you." She looked pointedly at her hand. "Are you trying to get us arrested?"

A hint of humor lit his eyes. "Am I disturbing you?"

"Yes."

"Good."

The waiter arrived with their drinks. "New in town?"

"Yes, we're here to visit my brother," Noah announced.

The waiter relaxed a fraction. "Uh, this isn't a great part of town for tourists," he told them. "Especially at night."

"Really? My brother mentioned this place," he told the waiter. "He eats here frequently."

The waiter looked perplexed again. "He does?"

"Yeah, he and some of his…friends. In fact, one guy, Jerome something or other, was killed in a bank holdup last week. You probably heard about that. My brother was pretty upset."

Sydney managed to keep her mouth closed, but she wondered why Noah was pretending to be someone else's brother.

The waiter relaxed. "Yeah. Jerome was a regular. Shame about what happened. That guy had it all, you know? Money, looks, charm, and he wasn't afraid to leave a good tip, if you know what I mean."

Noah held the man's gaze. "I know exactly what you mean. Have you seen Gunnar recently?"

Sydney tried not to jump at the name. The waiter's eyes narrowed, but then he shrugged. "I don't know any Gunnars. That your brother's name?"

"No, he's Barry," Noah said without hesitation.

Suspicion darkened the other man's expression. "Really?"

"Yeah, we're going to see him this afternoon."

The waiter smirked. "I guess that's why he took off out the back door when you came in just now."

"He did?" Sydney gasped.

Noah offered the man a smile. "He probably didn't think I'd told Sydney about his preferences. But you don't shock easily, do you, darlin'?"

Sydney pinched his thigh under the table. "Not since I met you, at any rate."

"We just got married," Noah put in.

The waiter rocked back on his heels. "Oh. That explains it. I know I heard Barry and Jerome mention your name."

"My name?" Sydney asked, suddenly frightened.

"Yeah, you know, in general conversation?"

Noah bristled. "How general?"

"Hey, easy man. We respect our customers' privacy here at Arnie's. Sydney's sort of an unusual name, you know? That's why I remember it. You don't have to go all alpha here. Sydney's not exactly their type, if you know what I mean."

His words didn't seem to soothe Noah.

"What people do behind closed doors is their business," Sydney told the waiter with a pasted-on smile. "Barry will discover I *don't* shock very easily."

"Hey, Lou," the bartender called out.

"Right there. Excuse me."

Noah turned and clasped her face, forcing her to look at him. "You're enamored of me, remember?"

"A little hard to forget." Her mind was whizzing past all the nuances of the conversation they'd just had, but one thing jumped out like a sore thumb. "Barry was just here, Noah! Shouldn't we go after him?"

Noah smiled at her, but his loving look was belied by the tension that practically radiated from his rigid frame.

"Absolutely not," he whispered, stroking her face for the audience. "First, we don't know for sure that Barry is the Barry Fairvale we met at the house. Second, if it is him and he was involved in that robbery, he's a cold-blooded killer. The only reason you're alive right now is because he wants that tape. At any point, he may decide to forget about it and make you his next victim."

If Noah had intended to scare her, he'd just succeeded. "Why did you pick his name when you were talking to the waiter?"

"It was the first one that came to mind. Maybe sub-consciously I recognized him when he jumped up and went out the back way."

"That could have backfired big time, Noah."

He shrugged. "You wanted information."

"Yes, but what do we do with it?"

"Drink your tea. We'll make plans once we get out of here."

Her mind was brimming with questions, and Noah was only confusing her further. She'd been trying to pretend last night had only been great sex. But she realized she'd never felt this connected to another person before. When Noah left, he'd take a large slice of her heart with him.

Outside, Noah hurried them back to the parking lot to retrieve the car.

"Was Jerome gay, Noah?" she asked as they drove away.

"Looks that way. I'm sorry, Syd."

She tossed her head. "Well, I'm not. Now I don't have to feel guilty that I never loved him."

Noah rested his hand on her thigh in answer. She smiled in response. Noah suddenly slammed on the brakes to avoid a stupid driver. Sydney had to retrieve the mail that sailed all over the floor.

A powder-blue envelope stopped her in midreach. She recognized it instantly. She'd purchased a package of colored envelopes by mistake one day. This had come from the same pack. The envelope was addressed to her at the apartment she'd shared with Jerome. And the handwriting was unmistakable.

"What's that?" Noah asked.

"It's addressed to me." Her hand began shaking. "Noah, that's Jerome's handwriting. It's dated the day before he died."

"Open it."

Carefully, she tore open the back flap and pulled out a single sheet of paper. A small key fell in her lap. Sydney tried to calm the wild beating of her heart as she unfolded the sheet of lined paper.

"'In case anything happens to me,'" she read aloud, "'this is the key to your safety deposit box. Don't tell anyone you have it.' He underlined the word *anyone* several times, Noah."

"Is that all it says?"

"No. He goes on to say, 'I'm sorry for everything. I'll make it all up to you, I promise. Jerome.'"

An invisible rock seemed to be pressing on her chest. Just when she thought she had her emotions under control, Jerome had to go and pull the plug again.

"The bastard," Noah muttered.

Sydney blinked.

"He put you at risk without a thought."

A car horn beeped imperiously. The traffic light had changed. Noah scowled and moved on.

Sydney realized he was right. Jerome had used her from the start. But in a way, she'd been using him, too, trying to capture the dream of a family that had lived in her heart.

"Let's go check out the safety deposit box," Noah said.

A MIX OF FEELINGS hit Sydney as soon as she started to walk inside the familiar building with Noah. The bank was busy since it was almost time to close. But Sydney pictured it as she'd last seen it. Empty. Eerie. Waiting for death.

Noah's hand reassuringly touched her shoulder. What was she going to do when he wasn't around to give her this silent support? She was coming to depend entirely too much on Noah.

She recognized most of the tellers, but there were also new people, including the assistant manager, who came forward to help them. A balding, heavyset man, he offered his condolences in a monotone, had her sign a card and led her to a small room across from the tellers. He returned a few minutes later with a surprisingly large box.

Her heart was beating so fast she was afraid she'd faint. With a shaking hand, she handed Noah the key. "You open it."

Noah framed her face in his hands. "You're a special lady, you know that?" He kissed her hard and fast. Before she could even savor the taste of him, he turned and unlocked the box.

Noah inhaled sharply. Sydney looked inside the open box. "My God, Noah!"

The box was packed with hundred-dollar bills. On top of one stack sat a tiny microcassette tape.

Noah lifted the tape gingerly and set it on the table. He riffled through the bills quickly. "That's it. Just the tape and the money."

"Just?" Her heart was pounding like a trip-hammer. "Noah, what was Jerome doing with all this money?"

Noah's expression confirmed the horrible truth.

"The bank robbery? But how?"

Noah shrugged. His eyes were dark with anger. "One of two ways that I can think of. He could have taken the money at closing the night before, knowing what was going to happen in the morning, or he could have come in earlier than anyone thought and helped himself before his accomplices showed up."

"The vaults are on a timer," she pointed out.

"But we don't know what time he told his accomplices to be here."

"He really was involved."

"Yeah."

"What do you think is on the tape?"

"Something that incriminates at least one or both of the men involved. Obviously, Jerome didn't trust them." He closed the box and turned the key. "Let's get out of here."

"What about the money?"

"We'll call Wickowski and let him handle things." He slipped the tape into his pants pocket and relocked the box. Minutes later they stood in the humid heat outside the bank.

Angry, dark clouds were closing rapidly on the horizon.

The air felt charged with primal energy—or maybe that was her emotions.

"You okay?" Noah asked.

"Just great. The father of my baby turned out to be a gay bank robber, but I'm fine. Don't I look fine?"

His eyes darkened more than the sky. Thunder boomed in the distance. The clouds rushed toward them on a blast of cool air.

"Sydney, about the baby—" Noah said sharply.

"What?"

"Jerome lied to you, Sydney. But this isn't a good time for this discussion. We need to call Wickowski."

"You can't just say something like that and change the subject, Noah."

He pointed to the fast-moving storm. "Do you want to stand here and wait for that to hit us?"

The sky was an ugly bruise of color, closing on them fast. Sydney looked at Noah's expression and decided now was not the ideal time to demand answers. Any more bad news and she'd probably snap.

"It's nearly two o'clock," she pointed out. "I doubt if he can get here before the bank closes."

"I'm more concerned that we get this tape in his hands before something else happens."

Sydney nodded at the shop next door. She'd worked in the small jewelry store for the past five years, yet it felt like a lifetime ago. "We could call him from Gioni's."

Noah scanned the parking lot tensely, then looked up as another rumble of thunder rolled overhead. "Okay."

There was a handful of customers inside. Mr. Gioni looked up with a happy smile when she walked in. "Sydney! It is so good to see you up and around again! You wait right there, okay? I'll be with you *un minuto*."

"We'd like to use the telephone if that's okay."

"Of course, of course. I will buzz you back."

"Thank you."

Sydney exchanged smiles with Ramona. The chubby clerk continued helping Mrs. Zettlemyer, an elderly lady who was a frequent customer.

Noah followed Sydney silently behind the display cases. She noticed him taking in the room and the people with military precision.

One look at her cluttered work station and Sydney yearned to be able to go back to work right then and there. If only she could make everything in her world return to what it had been before Jerome threw it into such utter chaos. She loved her work. She'd be lost without it. And if her hand didn't heal...

"The telephone is over there on the wall," she told Noah.

Sydney tuned out his conversation as she fingered her tools lightly. What did Noah know about her baby? The possibilities frightened her. Noah hung up and joined her, touching her lightly on the back.

"Wickowski was in his car. He's only a few minutes from here so he wants us to wait for him. Will you show me some of your designs while we wait?" he asked softly.

She wanted to question him, but it would be too reminiscent of the luncheon discussions she'd had back here with Jerome. "Most of my things are out front."

The store was growing dark as the storm approached. Mr. Gioni was still tied up with a middle-aged couple while Mrs. Zettlemyer dithered happily by the window over a pair of bracelets for her niece. Sydney offered Ramona a sympathetic smile as she led Noah to the case that displayed her more expensive designs.

"You do beautiful work," he said sincerely, rewarding her quiet pride. He pointed to one of her more expensive and personal favorite pieces. "That is absolutely stunning."

"So's the price tag," she told him.

"Oh my goodness! Look at that little boy," Mrs. Zettlemyer exclaimed. "His grandmother isn't watching."

They turned to the window in time to see a young tot give a sudden start at a loud clap of thunder and begin to run through the busy parking lot, screaming for his mother. An elderly woman with a cane turned around and set off in desperate pursuit.

"Oh, my goodness! That truck won't see him!"

"Stay here!" Noah ordered. He was out the door and running before Sydney could react to the horror playing out before their eyes. The frightened little boy ran toward them, right in the path of a large U-Haul truck that was slowly backing. There was no way the driver would ever see the small child.

Horrified, she saw Noah put on an amazing burst of speed. Lightning forked the sky and the first large drops of rain began to fall. He scooped the boy into his arms in plenty of time to prevent a tragedy. The U-Haul driver spotted Noah and came to a stop as the heavens split apart with a mighty deluge of rain.

The bell over the shop door tinkled. Sydney turned, shaking with relief, and came face-to-face with a man in a black ski mask. He aimed a gun at her face.

Déjà vu.

"Nobody move and no one will get hurt."

The woman beside Sydney gave a squeak of horror. Her husband pulled her against his chest. Ramona snaked her hand beneath the counter. Sydney knew the clerk had just activated the silent alarm.

"Give me the tape," the thief demanded.

Her mouth went dry with fear. She thought she detected the faint odor of garlic. "What tape?"

Thunder exploded overhead like a gunshot.

Sydney jumped. Without warning, the thief turned the gun toward Mr. Gioni and fired. The woman beside Sydney screamed. Her husband threw her to the floor beside a display case.

Ramona, too, dived beneath the counter. Mr. Gioni staggered back against a shelf of china figurines, blood staining his light gray suit coat from the hole in his shoulder.

"The next person who moves, dies. Now, give me the tape!" the man demanded, bringing the gun back in line with Sydney.

"I don't have any tape!"

"What did you get at the bank?"

He'd been following her? "We were talking to the new manager!" Would he know she was lying?

Before she could blink, he smashed the case at her side with his gun hand. He wore black leather gloves, she realized, and boots. Black pointed boots. The sort she associated with motorcycles and gangs. A snake tattoo wound its way up his arm.

"Grab some of the expensive stuff," he ordered.

Trembling, she reached into the case, cutting the back of her hand on a shard of glass. She ignored the cut, scooping up as many of the items as she could.

"Let's go."

He grabbed her arm and spun her toward the door. Her blood turned to ice. He planned to kill her. She knew it as surely as if he'd announced the deed.

He shoved her forward, practically pushing her through the front glass door. And the first thing she saw was Noah, running toward her. A police car suddenly tore into the lot, probably in response to the silent alarm. The thief fired, the shot deafening against her ear. The car screeched to a stop almost directly in front of them.

He fired at the police twice more, yanking Sydney back inside, shoving her against a display case. Jewelry fell from her hands. Wind and rain howled as lightning and thunder added to the chaos.

NOAH RETURNED the child to the sobbing grandmother, even as the child's terrified mother came running over. The horrified man driving the U-Haul thanked him profusely when a crack of thunder sent everyone running for cover.

As he turned toward the jewelry store, Noah spotted a large black motorcycle. Lots of people drove motorcycles. But Noah began to run all the same as the first of the rain began to fall.

A police car tore into the shopping center, squealing to a stop in front of the jewelry store. Noah had one second to see Sydney's terrified expression and the man who held her, before the hooded man opened fire. Sydney and her captor disappeared back inside out of sight as the wind drove a blinding rain wall of water straight at him.

"Get back!" The cop yelled at him.

Noah stopped. Charging into the situation unarmed wasn't going to do Sydney or anyone else any good. He tried to survey the scene analytically. It would take too long for Noah to explain to the cop who he was, and Wickowski would be here any minute.

The driving rain made it impossible to see inside the store. Noah set aside a wave of guilt for later. He blinked water from his eyes and pictured the people inside the jewelry store. Seven, counting the thief.

A second police car pulled into the shopping center.

Thankfully, Agent Wickowski was right behind him. Noah headed for the agent. As more police cars arrived and choked off the area, he explained what had happened.

The door to the jewelry shop opened abruptly. A little old lady was thrust forward, her hands over her head.

"Don't shoot! Don't shoot me! He says to let him go or he's going to start killing people! He shot Mr. Gioni!"

"We're going to call the store," an officer yelled back. "Tell him to—"

"No! He says no hostage negotiators and no SWAT teams! He wants to leave now or he's going to kill someone!"

Noah grabbed Wickowski by the shoulder. "He isn't bluffing."

Wickowski grunted. "According to the report I read, you're a trained marksman."

"Yes." His gut knotted. He knew what was coming.

"Can you take the guy out?"

"With someone else's weapon?"

Wickowski went to the trunk of his car. The clap of thunder all but obliterated the sound of the shot, but the little old lady collapsed like a boneless pile of rags onto the sidewalk.

Noah accepted the rifle.

The officer in charge objected strenuously when Wickowski and Noah approached. They had a SWAT team en route. They had hostage negotiators en route. They didn't want any interference. Wickowski didn't either.

The rain began to slow. A man suddenly appeared in the door of the shop. His face was pasty with fear as he called out in a shaken voice. "He says to let him go right now or he kills me. My wife will be next. For God's sake, do something!"

Noah moved up. He rested the barrel of the rifle on a

police car. He checked the sight. Using the rifle scope, he found the thief standing to one side of the man in the doorway.

He wasn't a clear target. The rain would affect the shot, and Noah had never fired this rifle before.

The man was using Sydney as a shield, a .gun to her head. If Noah fired, the thief's weapon could discharge, killing her. Noah needed an opening. Even then, he would have to make a head shot under impossible conditions.

And if he missed, he could kill Sydney.

Wickowski and the senior policeman approached. They were still arguing bitterly. Sydney was talking to the thief, anger and fear on her face. Noah blanked her from his mind. He drew on his training like a cloak. He blocked everything but those thoughts that centered on his target. The black ski mask was clearly silhouetted against the white wall, but the shot would be incredibly tight.

Then the gunman moved. Pulling Sydney along with him, he stepped closer to the door. That brought him closer to the window. He was agitated. Angry. One step. Two.

The thief straightened his arm, bringing the gun around toward the man in the doorway.

Between one heartbeat and the next, Noah fired.

Chapter Ten

The stench of his sweat practically suffocated her. The thief was scared and he was angry. Sydney had watched in horror as he shot Mrs. Zettlemyer in the back. Now he prepared to do the same thing to the man whose wife was sobbing uncontrollably.

Garlic breath yanked her forward two steps. He swung his arm out to fire again.

"No!" Sydney screamed. She wrenched to one side, trying to throw him off balance. Suddenly the man's wrist seemed to explode. The gun clattered to the floor. For a moment, shock held them all motionless. Then he yelled in pain while Sydney twisted free of his hold. She dived on top of the fallen gun.

Another shot exploded. Or maybe that was thunder. Sydney didn't know. She was deaf in one ear and her head was ringing from the sounds of the gunfire. The smell of sweat and garlic mingled with the scent of the cordite, making her ill. But she couldn't let him get the gun again no matter what he did.

The room erupted in noise and confusion. More gunshots. The thief fell beside her. A woman screamed shrilly, over and over, a horrible, loud grating sound. Sydney wanted to scream too, but she couldn't.

Male voices shouted. Hands reached for her. She curled tighter, struggling to protect the gun. Then she realized the hands belonged to a uniformed officer in a bright yellow slicker. The small display room was filled with wet angry people. And the thief lay where he'd fallen on the floor, unmoving. The policeman lifted her to her feet, urging her away.

Suddenly, Noah was there.

Sydney flung herself into his arms, dimly aware of his sodden clothing. She didn't care. She cared only that he was there, holding her tightly in his arms. She couldn't seem to stop shaking.

"Good shooting, Major."

Agent Wickowski's voice came from behind her.

"Your rifle pulls to the left and down," Noah told him. Wickowski grinned. "That was still one hell of a shot."

Sydney drew back. "You fired that shot?"

Noah looked bleak. "Only the first one."

She pulled his face to hers and kissed him fiercely, putting all the jumbled emotions she was feeling behind that kiss. After an instant, he kissed her back, hungrily, greedily, as if he couldn't get enough of her mouth. Which was exactly how she felt.

"I hate to break this up," Wickowski said, "but the media just arrived. If you two don't want to make the six o'clock report locked in a clinch, I'd save that stuff for later."

Reluctantly, Sydney stepped back. Noah loosened his hold, but he didn't release her.

"Mr. Gioni!" she remembered.

"He's with the ambulance attendants," Wickowski assured her, and she could see it was true. They had the shirt off his spindly body and were applying pressure to his wound.

"Looks like a flesh wound," Wickowski said.

"But what about Mrs. Zettlemyer?"

"Who?"

"She's a sweet little old lady, one of our steady customers. He made her go outside and then he shot her in the back to show you he meant business."

"Ah," Wickowski said with an understanding nod. "She's still alive. They took her away in the first ambulance."

"Thank God!"

"Yeah. We can all be thankful the guy was such a lousy shot. And that the major here wasn't."

Sydney saw someone had pulled away the gunman's mask. Barry Fairvale lay where he'd fallen. Two emergency medical technicians worked to stabilize him. They'd stripped away his shirt, revealing bloody holes in his chest and abdomen. That was what Noah had meant about a first shot. When Fairvale had run toward the door after Noah shot him, the police had fired until they brought him down.

The woman whose husband had come so close to being another victim abruptly collapsed in hysterics. Sydney glanced at Ramona. The clerk was shaken, but otherwise unharmed. In fact, she seemed to be taking events in stride now that the terror was over. She was certainly handling things better than Sydney, who was very glad that Noah continued to hold her.

"Come on," Wickowski said, "let's get the two of you out of here before the press is all over you like a cloudburst."

IT WAS EVENING before they found themselves back at Fools Point in Noah's father's house, with multiple cars in the driveway and two armed men in the kitchen.

"What would you say to a whirlpool bath?" Noah whispered in her ear.

"Yes."

He smiled and stroked her hair away from her face. Sydney had thought she was too tired to care about anything after they finished eating, but his touch proved her wrong. Her body came alive at his expression.

"Come on." They bade the two officers good-night and headed upstairs. "I'm not sure I've ever been that scared in all my life," Noah told her. "When I saw that gun pressed against your head—"

"I can't say it thrilled me much either. Did he follow us there, Noah?" She needed to touch and be touched. Probably some sort of affirmation of life after coming so close to death today. It would be so easy to love this man.

"He must have."

"What about the second bank robber?"

"Probably Coughlin or Yosten. Wickowski seems confident that Fairvale will tell them who he was if the tape doesn't. Did I mention the tub is big enough to hold two?" he added.

"No, I don't think you did."

While they made up the bed with fresh linens, Noah used every occasion to touch her, or give her warm, intimate looks that reminded her of their incredible lovemaking the night before.

"We can't do anything with those men downstairs."

"Of course we can. Their job is to see that we aren't disturbed tonight."

"I don't think that's how Agent Wickowski worded it."

"Same difference. And you did say something about needing a handmaid last night."

His slow sexy grin caused a hitch in her breathing. "If

you're applying for the job, I'll need references,'' she told him.

"Yeah?"

"Definitely."

"Beggars shouldn't be choosers. Remember,'' he pointed out triumphantly, ''now you can't get either hand wet."

"I can't?"

"Bandages."

She glanced at the small elastic strip on her left hand where she'd cut it on the display case. "Oh."

A river of wicked need flowed through her. No man had ever made her so completely aware of her own sexuality—or of his.

Raindrops pelted the window in a soothing rhythm. "I may not qualify as a handmaid, but I'm a pretty handy guy."

Her pulses danced with shimmering heat, hammering out a cadence her mind was just starting to understand.

"Hmm. How handy are you?"

He clasped her face between his hands. "Very, very handy."

Sydney stopped thinking entirely during the long, slow drugging kiss. A moan of need built in the back of her throat. The kiss turned demanding, but she wasn't sure which of them was doing the demanding. She couldn't get enough of him. Wanting was a fever straining outward from her very core.

When he eased back, his voice was as shaky and rough as she felt. "I'll wash your back,'' he offered in a low coaxing tone.

"My back?"

"And your front." He traced a finger over her collar

bone and down her chest, pausing just short of one beaded nipple. "And a lot of other interesting places."

His gaze smoldered. So did she. "At least we won't have to worry about bumps in the night tonight."

"Oh, I wouldn't say that, exactly." He raised his eyebrows suggestively and touched the tip of her nipple.

"I wasn't referring to that sort of bump."

"I'm not interested in any other kind."

Her body felt exquisitely tuned to his, ignited by the smallest touch, the least expression. She turned quickly before they ignited spontaneously, and checked out the bathroom.

"It is a large tub," she agreed, "but hardly large enough for two of us."

"Trust me. It's big enough." He turned on the taps, watching her through eyes that smoldered.

They shed their clothing in indecent haste before he turned on the jets and lowered her into the bubbling, foaming water. She scooted forward. He slid in behind her. Then he drew her against his chest. Pulling back her hair, he kissed the length of her neck, making her quiver expectantly. She twisted until their lips could meet, kissing him while his hands scooped water over her breasts, skimming her nipples until they were hard and pointed. Then he covered them with his rough palms. Her nipples responded almost painfully to his touch. It wasn't enough. Not nearly enough.

"Noah!"

His breath came in ragged pants. "I don't think I can wait," he said.

"Neither can I."

His fingers sank into her hips as he lifted her, positioning her, until with a single thrust, he was inside, filling her completely. She closed over him with demanding impatience, holding him inside her body.

With the water churning around them and his hands rubbing her sensitized breasts and his lips devouring her nip by erotic nip, Sydney stopped thinking altogether and gave herself over to the sheer physical pleasure of loving and being loved.

Her release, when it came, was savagely beautiful in its intensity. Noah drove to his own completion seconds later. She sagged limply against his chest in the foaming water, utterly spent.

"You are the most incredible woman I've ever known," he whispered against her hair.

"You're pretty spectacular yourself."

"Marry me, Sydney."

"What?" Her body tightened in shock, the mood dispelled in an instant.

"Marry me."

She reached over and turned off the jets, separating the two of them in the process. Water sloshed over the sides of the tub. "You can't be serious."

"Perfectly serious. I've never asked another woman to be my wife before."

Part of her instantly wanted to shout yes, but sanity prevailed.

"Don't shake your head," he objected. "I can take care of you, Sydney."

She bristled. "I don't need anyone to take care of me."

"Then you can take care of me."

He was serious. Fear chased away the peace of only moments ago.

"Noah, you know that's impossible."

"I don't know any such thing."

"We barely know each other."

His dark eyes seemed to look inside her soul. "We've been through one crisis after another. I'd say we know each other better than most couples."

There was some validity to that, but she shook her head once more. "I told you, I'll never rush into marriage again."

He drew his hand down her belly. Instantly, her body responded with awakening interest, despite the tremors his words were invoking.

"Not even for the sake of the baby?" he asked. "We could be married in three days. We'd be a real family."

He knew her fondest desire. She'd told him what that dream meant to her. And it was all too easy to picture Noah's role in her dream. "You aren't playing fair, Noah."

"I'm playing to win, Sydney. Marry me."

"I can't. You only think you want to marry me because of everything that's been happening to us. We've been thrown together during a terrible ordeal and—"

In one smooth motion he stood, bringing her with him. Water lapped at their legs. She felt ridiculous facing him naked in a tub full of water. But the moment her breast brushed his chest, another surge of wanton desire resurfaced.

She knew he correctly interpreted her reaction and triumph lit his eyes. "You still want me. Admit it. Give me that much at least, Sydney. Even though we just finished making love you still want me."

"That's a physical attraction, nothing more, Noah."

"Nothing? I'd say it's a lot more than nothing, Syd."

His mouth closed over hers. She tried not to respond, to stand quietly beneath the pressure of his lips, but it would have been easier to stop breathing completely. Just that fast, she wanted him all over again.

But he never once said the words that would have made everything right for her.

"Okay, you proved you can make me want you," she said when they drew apart, "but sex doesn't make a marriage, Noah."

"Maybe not, but it's a start."

Sydney climbed out of the tub and reached for a towel. She was sad and hurt and scared all at once. Her heart ached to accept all that he offered, but she couldn't. Sex wasn't love. And she'd already learned the hard way that without it, a relationship was nothing.

Noah stepped out of the tub and reached for a towel as well.

"There's something you have to know about the baby, Sydney."

Her hand flattened on her stomach. "What about the baby?"

"I've been trying to tell you for days, ever since I realized you didn't know the truth."

"You said Jerome lied," she remembered.

"He did. The baby isn't his. It's mine."

The world seemed to come to a stop, narrowing to just this man and his impossible words. Emotion punched a hole in her lungs, releasing all her air.

"No." The protest was a thin whisper of sound in a world without other noise. Suddenly cold and feeling naked and defenseless, she backed up, clutching the towel she had wrapped around her body.

"At first I assumed you knew, Syd. I waited at the hospital that morning for you to wake up so we could talk about the situation. Then I realized you had no clue."

His dark eyes watched her intently while his calm words turned her brain to ice.

"I thought you knew and agreed to my being the donor.

It was only when I asked to speak to Leslie that day at her office that I confirmed what I'd begun to suspect. Jerome tricked you. He tricked all of us. He altered the consent form you signed.''

"Why would he do that?"

"Jerome told me you were desperate to have a child—that you were threatening to leave him. Because of his low sperm count, he didn't even have a statistical chance of fathering his own child. He explained that neither of you wanted to take genetic chances, so he asked me to be the donor.''

"But why would *you* agree?"

Noah released his tension in a long sigh. "I never planned to marry, never planned to have children.''

"What does that have to do with anything?"

"It didn't seem like such a big request. Jerome and I weren't close. I never expected to meet you. Never expected to even see the child. He said I'd be saving his marriage, and at the same time, creating a way for our father's line to continue.''

She stared at him so bleakly, he felt sick. "How could you be so cold-blooded about creating a new life?"

Noah searched for an answer and couldn't find one. "I guess it just didn't seem very real. Everything seemed so simple when Jerome asked. You know how persuasive he could be.''

"Simple.'' She brushed her mouth with a knuckle. "So why bother to tell me now? Because it isn't *simple* anymore?''

"You deserved to know the truth.''

"Big of you to concede that fact now.''

"Syd, I tried to tell you before we made love the first time, remember?''

The sorrow in her eyes was eating a hole right through him. "You didn't try very hard, did you?"

"I know you're a little angry and upset right now—"

"Upset? You think I'm just a little upset?"

"Take it easy. You probably won't believe me, but I'm sorry."

"You're right, I don't. All this time we've been together. You made love to me—twice. Yet you couldn't tell me until now?"

His heart sank another notch. "I've been trying to tell you from the start. What do you want me to say, Sydney? I'm sorry." He held out his hand to touch her, but she backed away, her bottom lip quivering dangerously.

"No wonder you asked me to marry you. A good little soldier to the last, right, Major? Take care of your mistakes."

Her words lanced him. "You know better than that."

"Do I?" She shook her head, her damp hair swinging softly against her stricken face. Each word was a whiplash on his conscience, her expression so wounded it made him ache.

"I don't think I do, Major. But don't worry. As I told you all along, I can take care of myself. And I give you my word, I'll take very good care of *my* child."

She began picking up her clothes, trying awkwardly to dress with her one good hand, all the while shaking like a leaf in a gale. The strength of her anger surprised him. He knew she'd be upset, but he hadn't expected her to react so strongly. "Sydney, please. Calm down so we can talk."

"Leave me alone, Major. Just leave me alone."

Anger, hurt, betrayal. Her eyes swam with the mix of emotions swirling in their depths.

"Is that what you really want?"

"Yes."

"All right, Syd. I'll make up the bed next door. We'll talk after you calm down."

She clutched her clothing to her chest. A tear broke free and glided down her cheek but she raised her chin defiantly, anger sheeting from every muscle of her rigid body.

"Call me if you need anything," he said softly.

"Don't hold your breath."

IT WAS EARLY MORNING when Sydney heard the muted sound of breaking glass somewhere in the depths of the house. She'd spent hours crying into the pillow, and more hours struggling to come to terms with her emotions. In her calmer, more rational moments, she was enormously relieved that the child she carried wasn't Jerome's. But that Noah had taken part in the deception, however accidentally, with such casual disinterest hurt almost as much as the fact that he'd kept the truth from her for so long.

Her eyes burned from too much crying and too little sleep. She lay in the dark, silent bedroom and listened as another storm approached the house.

What was she going to do? There was no point lying to herself. She was in love with Noah, despite everything. But she could never marry him now, knowing she was just another obligation.

Without warning, the bedroom door opened soundlessly. A tall, dark figure slipped inside. Instantly, she tried to roll from the bed but before she could get free or scream he was across the room.

"Sydney!"

Her name hissed out of the darkness.

"Noah?" Relief surged through her followed by fresh anger. "What do you think you're do—?"

His hand clamped over her mouth. "No noise," he breathed in her ear. "Something's wrong."

The breaking glass, she realized. She would have thought her fear quotient had been used up for a lifetime by now. She would have thought wrong.

"Get dressed," he whispered, "but don't make a sound."

She wanted to yell and scream. To demand to know what was wrong. There were FBI agents downstairs. What could be wrong? But she obeyed him without question. Because she trusted Noah. He helped her pull on her shorts and top from the previous day.

"Someone was watching the house," he said so low she had to strain to hear him. "I started downstairs to alert the agents when I realized the lights were off down there. It feels wrong. I think he's inside, Sydney."

Horror threatened to give way to panic. "The agents?"

Noah shook his head. "I don't know what happened. Stay behind me and try not to make a sound. I'm getting you out of here."

Shivers racked her. She strained to hear the slightest sound, but all she could hear was the groaning wind, driving rain against the house.

A distant flash of lightning offered a small amount of illumination. Enough to orient her as they started down the steps. If they could make it down the stairs, they could go out the door before the intruder even knew they were on to him.

If they could make it down the stairs.

Noah reached the landing. The door leading to the back steps suddenly smacked his shoulder as it opened. She flattened herself against the wall as she caught a glimpse of a gun with a long barrel. Silencer, her mind supplied. There was a noise like a cough. Flame spouted from the barrel. Something thudded into the wall. Noah rammed the door against that arm. Then he flung it open, charging at the figure on the other side.

Locked together in a violent struggle, they fell down the back stairs into the kitchen. There was a grunt of pain and the gun coughed again. Her mind cried Noah's name. She bit her bottom lip to keep the sound inside. If he was okay, Noah would call out to her.

The house remained eerily silent.

Sydney knew what she had to do. She sprinted down the front stairs, running for the door.

"Sydney! Stop! I'll kill him!" The graveled voice held all the menace of a nightmare. "Right now! I mean it. He's dead if you don't stop."

He was on the back stairway, probably creeping back up to locate her. And she didn't doubt his words, not even for a minute. She hesitated, heart hammering wildly. She was three steps from the door and safety.

"All I want is the tape, Sydney. You and your lover can go free."

His voice was closer to the top of the landing. She had seconds to decide a course of action. Run or stay?

Every instinct said run. If Noah couldn't take out an armed man, she had no chance at all. She came down the last three steps, silently.

Noah might already be dead. She cringed from that possibility. Noah mustn't be dead. But he hadn't made a sound. She knew in her soul that he'd do anything he could to protect her. Therefore he couldn't.

She ran to the front door, fumbling with the dead bolt.

Feet pounded up the remaining back stairs. She flung open the door, but instead of running onto the porch, she dodged into the blackness of the living room. She stumbled and nearly fell when her foot struck something on the floor.

Lightning flared. Thunder trumpeted. She prayed it had blotted out the sounds she'd made.

As the footsteps pounded down the front stairs, she stood perfectly still, praying that no lightning flash would betray her.

He ran past, close enough to touch. As he went out the door, she bent, feeling for the object she'd just stumbled over. The cast-iron duck met her groping fingers. She clutched it, running for the kitchen. She nearly fell over Noah. He was sprawled on the kitchen floor at the foot of the staircase.

Her body clenched in horror as she reached for him in the darkness, desperately searching for a pulse. His hand snaked out and grabbed her arm. She gasped in startled horror, nearly dropping the cast-iron duck on his face.

"Sydney?"

"I thought you were dead."

Noah groaned. "Not quite. Where is he?"

"He thinks I ran out the front door."

"That won't fool him for long. Help me up."

"How bad are you hurt?"

"I'm still alive. Shhh."

She didn't know what he heard, but dread gripped her. He pulled her face down near his mouth. "Go to the cellar. Hide. Now!" And he pushed her away. The shove nearly toppled her.

Sydney didn't waste time arguing. She wasn't about to descend into some dark, unknown basement. Besides, she didn't even know which door led to the basement. She stood and moved to the wall beside the opening that led to the dining room.

Holding her breath, she strained to hear. The intruder bumped into something in the living room. The sound was small, but enough to fix his position.

She had never been so terrified in all her life. She sensed Noah's frustration that she hadn't obeyed him, but she couldn't. Instead, she flattened herself against the smooth surface of the wall and waited. The cast-iron duck became an unbearable weight in her shaking hand, but she gripped it all the tighter, knowing it was the only chance they had. She had to hit him, and hit him hard enough to knock the gun out of his hand or she and Noah would die.

She actually smelled him before she heard him again. He stank of sweat and rain and turpentine. His wet shoes squished as he crept closer to the kitchen. He couldn't know for sure that she was still inside. More likely, he'd decided to check on Noah. To be sure of at least one of them.

Noah didn't move. Sydney didn't even breathe. She sensed the intruder standing just short of the opening. Terrified to the point of passing out, she willed him to take that last step that would bring him into range.

Lightning and thunder exploded overhead. He took that final step forward. She brought the duck down with all the strength in her body, hitting his arm. Bone cracked with a loud snapping sound. He screamed in primal rage and pain. The duck fell from her nerveless fingers and landed on his foot. He yelled once more.

As he turned toward her with a bellow of sheer rage, Noah came to life. He lashed out with his legs, catching the man at the back of his knees. The gun flamed. Sydney would have sworn she felt the bullet tear past her face. It slammed into the wall at her back.

Then the gun fell to the floor, skittering across the linoleum as the two men began to struggle. Sydney tried to stay out of the way, unable to tell who was where in the tangle of arms and legs.

When she saw her way clear, she darted into the dining room. She hit the wall switch, bringing the ancient chandelier to life.

Gunnar Yosten slammed his left hand into Noah's face. She recognized him instantly, even though she'd only seen him that one time from a distance.

He drew back his fist to strike again and she reached for the duck, intending to bring it down on his head. Noah, however, struck the arm she'd broken. Gunnar screamed and suddenly collapsed. He didn't move.

A gust of wind shook the entire house.

"Is he dead?"

Noah shook his head. "I think he passed out."

Thunder boomed overhead. Rain pelted the house. Sydney couldn't stop the gut-wrenching shivers that ran through her body.

Gunnar's arm lay at an impossible angle. Something white stuck out of the skin above his wrist. She realized it was the bone. For a moment, she thought she'd vomit. Then she got a good look at Noah. His chest was awash in red blood. It matted his chest hair and stained his arms. There was so much blood.

"Oh my God, Noah!"

He leaned back against the steps, his face stark with pain. She set the duck on the kitchen counter and hunted for the wall switch. The kitchen flooded with brilliant light. Noah's face was pale as death in the bright illumination. There was a rattling sound when he drew in a breath. She looked around wildly and spotted the body slumped over the kitchen table, a shattered glass still in his hand.

"Get...the gun." Noah said weakly. "If he moves, shoot him."

Sydney swallowed hard against the nausea swelling in her throat. She was literally sick with fear. He was bleeding so badly. She reached for the gun, despite her horror of the weapon, and thrust the handle at Noah. He gripped it limply. He looked as if he were going to pass out any moment. He mustn't pass out. She didn't know enough first aid. He had to help her. Tell her what to do.

"Don't you *dare* pass out, do you hear me, Noah Inglewood? Don't you *dare!*"

"Syd—"

"Hold that damn gun! I mean it, Noah! I cannot do this. You hold that gun and you shoot him if he moves. I have to stop the bleeding. Do you understand? Don't you move!"

Her voice was a shrill screech. The entire court should be able to hear her yell.

Noah managed a wry curl of his lips. "Always... knew...you were bossy."

"That's right. And don't forget it. What kind of hero goes and gets himself shot?"

"Care...less one."

She tore open drawers, yelling at him the entire time to keep him from passing out. Finally, she found the one with a stack of clean dish towels. She pulled them out, sticking several under the water to wet them down, then she knelt beside him, gently wiping at the blood until she found the open wound.

Noah's breathing was getting worse. She was pretty sure he had a collapsed lung at the very least. He needed help and he needed it now. She had to go for a telephone. But she couldn't leave him here. Especially not with Gunnar.

"Syd. I'm not…going to stay conscious much longer."

"Yes, you are. You have to. Do you hear me?"

"I think…heaven's…probably wearing earplugs."

He tried to laugh and began to cough. Red spittle dotted his lips.

"Then they'd better listen harder. Don't you dare die on me, Noah. I love you, you stupid foolish man. I'm going for help. Please don't die, Noah." She could feel the tears burning her eyes. "Please. I need you. Our baby needs you."

His lips curved in a smile. His eyes closed and he didn't move. Sheer unadulterated terror gripped her. She felt for a pulse. He was still alive. She took the gun from his limp hand and ran for the back door. Throwing it open, she raced outside and fell over the second agent. He was face-down on the porch and he wasn't moving either.

She spun, seeking lights to guide her. Wind and rain whipped at her hair and clothing. The lights were on in the house next door so she plunged across the sodden grass, slipping once and skinning her knee. Then she was up and running again, scrambling on their back porch, pounding on the door and screaming for help as loud as she could.

A porch light went on over her head. A man opened the door and gaped at her.

"I need an ambulance! Next door. The Inglewood house. Tell them Noah's been shot. The FBI men were shot and I think they're both dead. Noah's bleeding to death. Hurry! The gunman could wake any minute. They have to hurry!"

She waved her arms, only then realizing she still held the gun.

"John? What is it? Who's at the door?"

The man called John turned toward the woman's voice

and Sydney took off, back across the grass that separated the two properties. She paused beside the fallen agent, but in a flash of light she saw he was beyond her help. Sydney charged into the kitchen and came to a stop. The man at the table hadn't moved either, but Noah was slumped over, his face practically in his lap—and Gunnar Yosten was gone.

"Oh, God!"

She took two faltering steps forward, rain streaming down her face, and the door to the left of her swung open. Gunnar stood there, pointing another gun at her head. His broken arm dangled uselessly at his side. Beads of moisture dotted his face, which was contorted in pain. His hair was wet and flat to his head and his eyes were filled with hate.

"Where is the tape?" he demanded.

Was it possible he didn't know the FBI had his partner and the tape? Almost, she told him the truth. "It's in the safety deposit box at the bank. You'll never get it without me, and if you kill me, the police will find it along with the money."

"What money?"

"There's thousands of hundred-dollar bills in the box along with the tape."

His eyes glowed with beady intensity. "That bastard."

"Yes. Jerome was definitely that."

"Put the gun down," Gunnar ordered.

"No."

His cold eyes narrowed. His finger rested on the trigger. Sydney hadn't known it was possible to be this scared and not faint. But she knew if she obeyed Gunnar now, he'd kill her. He had to know the whole thing was coming apart. He had nothing to lose by killing the only eyewitness, and he just might figure her death would buy him some time. She brought the barrel up, pointing it at the middle of his chest.

"Do you think you can pull that trigger, Sydney?"

"I know I can," she told him. And she realized she meant it. She would do whatever it took to try and save Noah and her child. "I told the next-door neighbor to call the police. I used your name and Noah's when I spoke to him. By now, he's already called it in. The police station is right down the road. You've got one chance. Run and keep running."

"And maybe you're lying."

"You know I'm not."

They both heard the sound of the siren. He looked from her to the open door. The thunder was moving away, but it was still loud enough to make her jump. She saw in his cold blue eyes, the moment he made his decision. He was going to shoot her.

She squeezed the trigger. The gun jerked in her hand. Simultaneously, his smaller gun spat a stream of flame in her direction. Something thudded into the wall behind her, and a small round hole appeared in his forehead. Gunnar Yosten looked right at her. Then his eyes went blank and he pitched forward.

Sydney screamed. She thought she glimpsed someone on the back porch, but feet were running through the house toward her and a voice yelled, "Police! Drop your weapon!"

Chapter Eleven

"Okay, Sydney. You can sit up and get dressed now," Dr. Leslie Martin told her. "Everything is progressing nicely. For now."

"What do you mean, for now? What's wrong?" Sydney sat up on the examining table and pushed the hair back from her face.

The doctor eyed her critically. "I have seriously ill patients who look better than you do. I spoke with your surgeon the other day and he says you've started physical therapy. He thinks you'll make a full recovery. The baby is fine. So I can think of only two problems causing those bags under your eyes. You aren't sleeping because you had to kill Gunnar Yosten, or you aren't sleeping because you haven't seen Noah since they moved him to Walter Reed. Do you want to talk about it?"

The temptation to confide in the doctor was strong. She liked Dr. Martin and she needed someone to confide in. Laura had taken a new job in Kansas to be closer to her family, while Hannah was so much in love with her new husband that Sydney felt uncomfortable in her friend's company.

As a result, Sydney had felt lost ever since walking out

of Noah's hospital room more than a week ago, when they told her he would make it. The FBI agents hadn't been as lucky and she'd shed several tears for them and their families.

Sydney had been staying at the house in Fools Point, first because it was closer to the hospital where they'd initially taken Noah, then because her things were there and she had nowhere else to go. She'd closed up Jerome's apartment, and with Laura gone, she wasn't comfortable staying at her old apartment.

"Actually, I didn't kill Gunnar Yosten," she told the doctor. "According to Chief Hepplewhite, my shot went into a cupboard. A police officer on the back porch fired the fatal bullet."

"That must make you feel better."

Sydney shook her head. "I keep thinking if he hadn't arrived when he did, we'd both be dead."

"I can give you something for the nightmares, Sydney."

"I'd rather not. It isn't good for the baby. I can deal with them."

"Not from where I'm standing, but it's up to you. If you change your mind, let me know. I understand they've recovered all the money."

"Yes. They discovered Jerome had a second safety deposit box at the bank. They found his personal papers and another tape he made of them planning the crime. Gunnar was the brains, while Barry selected the easiest employee to exploit. They seem certain no one else was involved."

"I'm glad it's finally over. I saw Noah this morning," the doctor said carefully. "They're going to discharge him from the hospital tomorrow."

The doctor closed her chart and tapped her pen against

the cover while Sydney absorbed her words. "You know, you're my last patient today. Jasmine left early. How would you like a glass of iced tea? It's decaffeinated."

"I'd like that. Thank you." She wasn't in a hurry to be alone with her own thoughts again right now.

"Call me Leslie. I know I'm your doctor, but I'd also like to be your friend."

"I'd like that, too."

Leslie shut off the lights and locked down the office. She led Sydney through a door at the end of the hall and into a bright, cozy kitchen.

"Have a seat," she said, heading for the refrigerator. "Feel free to tell me to butt out, if you'd like, but what happened between you and Noah?"

Sydney sat at the table and began toying with the bright teal and yellow place mats while Leslie pulled out glasses and a pitcher of tea. The hurt was a dull ache in her chest.

"Noah told me he's really the father of my baby."

Leslie nodded. She poured tea into both glasses and sat down. "I thought that might be the problem."

"He said he inadvertently made you an accomplice in the fraud."

"Yes. What Jerome did was highly illegal. You know about the informed consent law."

Sydney nodded. "All those papers I had to fill out agreeing to have the procedure done."

"That's right. While I wasn't directly involved in the deception, I agreed to let Noah ship the sperm here for Jerome to pick up. I didn't know you were in the dark about the real donor. That's illegal."

"Are you going to get in trouble?"

"That depends. Are you going to prosecute?"

Shocked, Sydney stared at her. "Of course not."

Leslie nodded. "I didn't think so. Do you love Noah?"

Sydney didn't have to think about her answer. "Yes. When he was shot I..." There weren't words to express the devastation she'd felt. Even her grandma's death, leaving her alone in the world at sixteen, hadn't left her as scared or as empty in her heart.

"It's okay. I can imagine. Noah's doing great, I'm happy to report. A child should have both his parents."

Sydney frowned. "We're not getting married."

"Why not?"

Sydney thought of all the reasons she could give and then settled on the only one that really mattered. "He doesn't love me. The baby and I are just a responsibility."

Leslie paused, the glass halfway to her lips. Finally, she closed her mouth over the rim, took a swallow and set the glass back down. With a toss of her head she said, "I know they say love is blind, but this is ridiculous. Sydney, that man is head over heels in love with you."

Her heart began to race. "You're wrong. He never once said that."

Leslie pursed her lips and raised her eyes toward the ceiling. "I've known Noah since grade school. That man loves you more than you know. Men like Noah don't bother with words. People use them without real meaning. Noah's the type to show you how he feels, in ways that count."

Sydney pictured Noah rushing into danger—almost dying. Holding her when she was frightened. Making exquisitely tender love to her.

Leslie set her glass down with a decided thunk. "Think long and hard before you let Noah walk out of your life."

"I don't want him out of my life," she admitted. "Or out of the baby's life."

"Good, because he'll make a wonderfully loving father if you give him a chance. Trust me, I'm usually right about this sort of thing."

"Even if he does love me, he's already wedded to his military career."

Her eyebrows disappeared under her bangs as Leslie looked up at the ceiling again and shook her head. "Ever hear of divorce?"

SYDNEY THOUGHT about that discussion as she tossed in the large king-size bed that night. She'd gotten past most of her hurt the minute she saw Noah bleeding to death. The problem was, she didn't want to make another mistake. What if Leslie was wrong? What if Noah didn't love her after all? What if his sense of duty and responsibility were the only reasons he'd proposed to her?

Giving up the fruitless battle for sleep, she rose before the sun and cleaned house, needing something to occupy her time. She thought of the FBI agents Gunnar had murdered. They would never see their children grow. And she thought of Noah. Of his blood spilling onto the kitchen floor. And she wondered why she was being such a fool.

"I DON'T NEED or want a wheelchair," Noah said flatly.

"Yes, sir, I understand that, but—"

"Intimidating the troops, Major?"

Noah jerked his head in the direction of the door, shocked to see Sydney standing there. He feasted his eyes over every inch of her. She wore a loose-fitting cotton sundress and there were dark circles under her eyes that makeup couldn't cover. But seeing her was balm for his soul.

"I'll handle him," Sydney told the woman standing behind the wheelchair.

"Uh, yes, ma'am." The young woman scurried from the room.

"She's not one of the troops, she's a civilian," Noah told Sydney. "And I think you're the one who intimidated her."

"Maybe so, but I did it with less aggression."

"Is that right?"

Her skin was pale, and she obviously hadn't been sleeping. He could relate to that. He'd been going frantic worrying about her for the past week.

"I wasn't expecting you," he said.

She didn't smile. "I thought you might need a lift home."

"Home?"

"To Fools Point."

He stared, trying to decide why she was here. He was afraid to let himself believe what he so desperately wanted to believe. "I was planning to go and look for you."

"Really?" She licked her lips. Sydney was nervous. That surprised him, but it also eased a knot of tension in his chest.

"I've been practicing my groveling," he told her.

"Oh?"

"I figure there's no way an apology will cut it, so I'm going to have to throw myself at your feet and beg."

Her wonderfully soft lips began to curl with the hint of a smile.

"There's something about that image I really like, Major."

"I had a feeling it would appeal to you." He took a

step closer and caught the faintest trace of gardenias. "I always knew you were officer material."

"You would know."

He stepped close enough to touch her, but he didn't. "Is there any way to fix the broken trust between us?"

Her gaze never wavered, but he couldn't tell what she was thinking. Was she willing to forgive him or was she going to suggest he get himself stationed somewhere like Alaska?

"You could marry me," she said softly.

A crushing weight lifted from him. Noah opened his arms. She came into them without hesitation. Warmly, softly—his. He let her scent envelop him and held her tightly, still terrified that she would pull away.

"I'm sorry, Syd," he said, breathing against her soft hair.

"I know. It's okay. It just took me a while to get things right in my mind." She pulled her face back to stare into his eyes. "Leslie was right. You're going to make a terrific father."

He crushed her against his chest and covered her lips, letting his kiss speak for him.

They were both breathing heavily when they pulled apart.

"I love you, Sydney."

"I know that, now. Why don't you get in the chair, Major, and we'll go home and discuss plans for the rest of our lives."

"I like the sound of that, but I don't need a wheelchair," he told her.

"I'm pulling rank. The woman hiding in the corridor says you do. Are you going to argue over a stupid wheelchair, or are you going to save that energy for something more productive?''

Noah climbed into the wheelchair. ''I've got a feeling the next seventy years or so are going to prove an interesting challenge.''

''Count on it, Major.''

Award-winning, best-selling author
Rebecca York
returns to
Silhouette Intrigue™
in September with her latest
43 LIGHT STREET
novel,

Amanda's Child

Here's a sneak preview…

Amanda's Child

by

Rebecca York

After pulling the vehicle as far as she could into a small grove of trees, she climbed out and looked up into the star-filled sky, the twinkling points of light making her feel very small and very unprotected. In her nightgown the chill air raised goose bumps on her skin.

She wanted to get back to Matt, and the sudden feeling of dependence brought a flash of self-doubt. For years she prided herself on being able to handle anything that came along—even her father's final illness. In the space of a few hours she'd started to rely on Matt Forester.

Or maybe that wasn't what she was feeling, she told herself as she scrambled for a better explanation. Maybe she was reacting this way because she felt responsible for what had happened to him since he'd been injured by *her* foreman. In spite of that, a little while ago, he'd kissed her, and she'd tasted as much need in his kiss as passion.

If he'd been in better shape—or if she'd had more experience communicating with men—she might have marched back to the cabin and demanded to know exactly what that kiss had meant. But she wasn't sure he would even know the answer—not when he was half out of his head, courtesy of her foreman.

So she worked off some of her frustration by scooping up several handfuls of fallen leaves and scattering them over the roof and the hood of the vehicle. Standing back, she swiped her hands together to dust away the bits of clinging leaf and surveyed her handiwork. Maybe the covering would disguise the shiny surface—if someone did decide to investigate this place from the air.

After retrieving the gun and her purse, she started back to the cabin. But one of the annoyances of pregnancy stopped her. Unfortunately these cabins out in the middle of nowhere didn't come equipped with bathroom facilities. So she checked the tissue supply in her pocketbook and made a strategic stop in a convenient thicket.

Back in the cabin, she laid the gun within her reach, then knelt and touched Matt's shoulder, tensing as she imagined him lunging at her again. But this time he only opened his eyes and gave her a lazy smile.

"You're feeling better," she murmured.

"Mm-hmm."

"I should check your pupils with the flashlight. I should have done that before."

He winced. "Do you have to?"

"You know I do."

She reached for the light, switched it on and

directed the beam towards his face. He sucked in a sharp breath as the brightness hit him, but both his pupils contracted the same amount.

"Do I pass?" he asked, rubbing his eyes as she switched off the light.

"Yes." *Thank the lord*, she added silently.

"Then lie down and get some sleep. You're going to need it."

She looked around the cabin and back at the makeshift bed. "Lie down with you?"

"I'm in no shape to start anything."

"Aren't you?" she asked, remembering the potency of his kiss. What was he like when he *was* in shape?

"I won't do anything out of line. Promise." When she didn't move, he added, "You must be dead on your feet by now." Holding up the top blanket, he waited for her decision.

Perhaps the trembling of his hand was the deciding factor. Or maybe she was too tired to think straight, too tired to run any farther—from Roy Logan or from the man who'd kidnapped her and was now offering to share his bed.

Without understanding why she trusted Matthew Forester on such a basic level, when wariness was such an ingrained facet of her personality, she eased onto the blanket and rolled to her side, her face away from him.

* * *

Don't forget Amanda's Child *is a September Silhouette Intrigue*™

▼™SILHOUETTE
INTRIGUE™

AVAILABLE FROM 17TH AUGUST 2001

SAFE BY HIS SIDE Debra Webb

No-one could find special agent Jack Raine if he didn't
want to be found. So how did a beautiful amnesiac end up
on his doorstep with a killer close on her heels? 'Kate'
couldn't remember her own name but she wanted Jack the
moment she saw him—a man her flashes of memory
suggested she might have been sent to capture…

THE BODYGUARD'S ASSIGNMENT Amanda Stevens

Texas Confidential

When Brady Morgan had to protect beautiful witness
Grace Drummond until she testified, their passionate past
came back to haunt him. Grace was desperate to avoid
testifying, but could she trust Brady with the reason? With
a killer on their trail and desire boiling beneath the
surface, Brady would need all his expertise to keep Grace
alive—and in his arms…

AMANDA'S CHILD Rebecca York

43 Light Street

Amanda Barnwell had no choice but to trust her
handsome kidnapper, Matt Forester. He swore he was
saving her from the family of the sperm-donor who had
fathered her unborn child—a family who would stop at
nothing to claim the baby, including eliminating Amanda.
But was Matt telling the truth?

JUST ONE LOOK Mary McBride

Coming around after being attacked, the first person Sara
Campbell saw was detective Joe Decker. Sara was the one
living witness to a killer's face, *if only she could remember!*
Which meant this rugged cop had to protect her from
danger…*all day and all night!*

0801/46a